Constant Craving

Task Force Hawaii Book Three

Melissa Schroeder

Edited by
Noel Varner

Cover Art by
Scott Carpenter

Harmless Publishing

Also by Melissa Schroeder

The Camos and Cupcakes World

- Camos and Cupcakes
- The Fillmore Siblings
- Juniper Springs

The Santini World

- The Santinis
- Semper Fi Marines
- The Fitzpatricks

The Harmless World

- The Harmless Series
- A Little Harmless Military Romance
- Task Force Hawaii

Check out the rest of Mel's books by:

- Interest
- Series
- Entire Backlist

About Constant Craving

She might trust him with her life but she's not too sure she can trust him with her heart.

Charity Edwards has never been a woman who liked to compromise–not at work and definitely not in her personal life. So, when TJ Callahan appears on the scene as their FBI liaison, she decides to take a chance on the slow talking Texan.

TJ doesn't like undercover work, but thanks to an old case, he has been tasked to do just that. He uses his position to infiltrate TFH to investigate Charity, a woman well-known for her hacking skills. His almost instant attraction he has to Charity makes it impossible not to blur the lines and he soon finds himself falling for the impossible woman.

When his assignment is revealed, Charity wants nothing to do with him, but she has no choice. Thanks to TJ's investigation, Charity's life is in jeopardy and he will do anything to protect her–even if it means sacrificing himself.

Especially for Noel Varner.
Your boundless energy and constant support makes editing not such a crappy experience.

ABOUT TASK FORCE HAWAII

Even paradise has a dark side...

Working with local, state, and federal agencies, the men and women of TASK FORCE HAWAII work on cases ranging from bank heists to terrorism. A diverse team filled with ex-military, law enforcement, medical, and technical support, they are Hawaii's last defense against the worst criminals.

If you want to know more about the book, characters, and places described, check out the TFH Pinterest boards!

Task Force Hawaii
Seductive Reasoning
Hostile Desires
Constant Craving
Tangled Passions
Wicked Temptations
Twisted Emotions

MEET THE TEAM

CAPTAIN
Martin "Del" Delano

Second in Command
Lt. Adam Lee

Regular Team Members
Graeme McGregor
Marcus Floyd
Cat Kalakaua

Medical Team
Dr. Elle Middleton
Drew Franklin

Forensics
Charity Edwards

Contractors
Emma Taylor

Help with Hawaiian Terms

Aloha - Hello, goodbye, love
Bra-Bro
Bruddah- brother, term of endearment
Haole-Newcomer to the islands
Howzit - How is it going?
Kamaʻāina-Local to the islands
Mahalo-Thank you
Malasadas- A Portuguese donut without a hole which started out as a tradition for Shrove (Fat) Tuesday. They are deep fried, dipped in sugar or cinnamon and sugar. In other words, it is a decadent treat every person must try when they go to Hawaii. If you do not try it, you fail. Do yourself a favor. Go to Leonard's and buy one. You are welcome.
Slippahs - slippers, AKA sandals

Constant Craving

Copyright © 2016 by Melissa Schroeder
Published by Harmless Publishing

All rights reserved.
No part of this book may be reproduced in any form or by any electronic or mechanical means, including information storage and retrieval systems, without written permission from the author, except for the use of brief quotations in a book review.

First digital publication: May 2016

This is a work of fiction. Names, characters, places and incidents either are the product of the author's imagination or are used factiously and any resemblance to actual persons living or dead, business establishments, events or locales is entirely

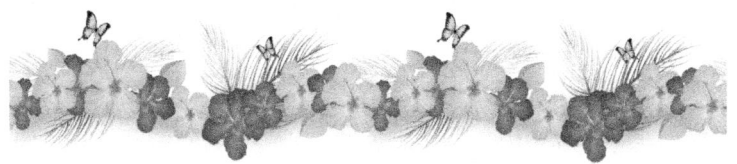

Chapter One

Charity Edwards stretched her hands over her head and sighed. Taking Friday off had been a good idea. She had a lot of leave time, plus, her boss Del instituted a payback time policy. He believed they should take advantage of the slower times because there were periods that would have them working around the clock.

And this was definitely a slow time. It had been close to two full weeks since they'd had a case, and all of them were getting antsy. Task Force Hawaii handled high profile cases, and many ended up dragging on for weeks and involved several local, state, and federal departments. At the moment though, there was an eerie calm about their work. With each day that passed without a new case, the unnatural atmosphere worsened and all of them were on edge. None of them wanted to admit it, but it felt as if something was coming to get them.

She shook her head. Her mama always said she had an active imagination. Staying up late watching horror movies last night had been a bad idea.

Slipping out of bed, she decided to get some coffee and enjoy the morning views. After a quick trip to the bathroom, she made her way to the kitchen. She was a caffeine junky and needed it to be able to function. And not kill people. That was something that it helped with. After brewing a single cup, she headed out to her lanai.

She sipped her coffee and watched the busy traffic below. Then, she looked out toward the direction of Diamond Head. The sun was just starting to peek over the buildings, casting light and shadows on a city she was starting to adore.

Georgia was a far cry from her sixteenth floor apartment in Capitol Center in downtown Honolulu, or even the townhouse she'd had in Georgetown when she'd lived in DC. She missed what she had always thought of as home, but now, in less than a year, she had come to fall in love with the Hawaiian Islands, their customs and people.

Just thinking about Georgia made her think of her parents. An only child of only children, they had a small meddlesome family. Her mother liked to say that they all just knew each other better than most, Charity thought with a smile. She would give anything for one of her mother's cinnamon rolls. Celeste Edwards knew how to make the most amazing sweets, and Charity had the hips to prove it.

"Morning," Drew Franklin mumbled as he stepped out on the lanai.

She glanced at him. It had been six months since the shooting that almost took his life. He looked better, but he wasn't truly fine. She knew that better than anyone. About a month ago, she'd made him move into her spare room. She had planned on making it her walk-in closet—and yes, she did have that many clothes—but she knew that Drew needed to live with her for a while. Otherwise, he would have stayed at his folks' place and hidden from everyone. At least this way, she could force him out every now and then.

"Morning, champ."

He sat down in the other chair and looked out at the city. He had always been one of the most positive people she had known. She could always count on him to cheer her up with an absurd joke or his observations on life. That is, until the shooting. Now, he was grumpy most of the time. Part of it was the pain, the other part of it was their teammate Cat. Their romance had withered after the shooting, and Charity wasn't sure if they had actually talked since he'd left the hospital. She knew he hadn't been back to work, so there was a good chance they hadn't had a conversation.

Luke and Jess, her two cats, slunk out onto the lanai. She had grown up with dogs. Lots of them, and she loved them—along with most animals. But with her hours, and the fact that she lived in an apartment, she thought it best to stay with cats for the moment. Of course, they hated every single person on the face of the earth except her. That is, until Drew had moved in. They had taken to sleeping with him.

"Are you planning on heading out to your folks' place today?"

He shrugged, as Luke jumped into Drew's lap. Luke was a Himalayan she had rescued from behind her first apartment in Hawaii. He stared at her across the table with the most irritated look. Not to be ignored, Jess jumped into her lap and purred. Charity knew that she had been Jess' second pick. The American short-haired/tiger mix stared at Drew, coveting him as she allowed Charity to pet her.

"I thought we could pop on by and see everyone. Get out. Get lunch somewhere since you won't cook for me."

He grunted. She hated that sound. And, at one time she let it go. He'd died twice on the operating table, and they had all handled him with kid gloves. She was thinking now might be time to take them off.

"Yes. We will go out."

"I thought you said you took off to sleep in. You're up earlier than you get up on a regular work day."

"When I have to get up for work, I don't want to get up. Don't try to distract me. We're going out today and have fun."

He slunk down further in his chair. That was his only response. She could give him space, even let him be a pain in the ass for a while. Acting like a sullen teenager was a little too much.

"No way out of it, Andrew Franklin. We are going out and you will get some sun. It will be good for you."

Without waiting for his reply, she stood up and hurried off to get ready. The best thing her mama ever taught her was to just steamroll men. Don't give them time to think. Men always created too many problems when they thought too much.

She grabbed another cup of coffee and headed off to her bedroom. Today was going to be a glorious day.

FBI Agent TJ Callahan was shutting down his computer as Freddy Santos came walking by his office. The California transplant had been TJ's sponsor when he moved to Hawaii less than a year ago.

"Hey, Hammer. Boss wants to see you."

Damn. This close to freedom. "Why?"

Freddy shrugged. "I was in his office and your old supervisor called in. Said he needed you right now."

Fuck. He hated meetings. He especially hated to have anything to do with DC. He'd left a year ago, and he hadn't regretted it one bit. But, overall, meetings sucked. They always took too long and were a lot of wasted time. They could accomplish what needed to be done in about half the time. TJ knew it was a bad thing to be called into the supervisor's office on a Friday. They might be the FBI, but they were in Honolulu. Officially, they were still at work, but late on a Friday afternoon, the Aloha Friday spirit was alive and well—even in their office.

With regret, he watched many of his coworkers, including Santos, start to head to the elevators. Aloha Friday was definitely upon them, and the lucky bastards were getting a head start. TJ could almost taste the Longboard Ale he had chilling in his fridge at home. He closed his eyes and licked his lips.

"Callahan," his boss bellowed from down the hall.

TJ opened his eyes and decided to pay the piper. The sooner he could get done with that, the sooner he could get to work at home. Since buying his house a few months ago, he had relished his weekends. No more eighty-hour work weeks for Agent Callahan. No way. Here, he left early on Fridays and spent his weekends surfing and refurbishing his house in Waimanalo.

Sighing, he stood and made his way to Agent Tsu's office. Since TJ's transfer, things had been easy. He did most of his work at his desk, where he was most comfortable. It was something he had insisted upon after the FUBAR in DC. His last assignment had gone south, and he'd been in the hospital for a week afterwards. He did not want to go through that again.

TJ stepped into Tsu's office and saw his former boss on the big screen.

"Hey, Hammer. How's it going?" Agent Remington said.

Remington was a hell of a guy, and had been a kick ass boss. He had been one of the first agents assigned to cyber terrorism back in the day. Working for him had been one of the highlights of TJ's career so far. Unfortunately, it had brought about some very bad times as well.

Fifteen years older than TJ, Stan Remington showed his age in the fine wisps of grey littering his dark brown hair. But his face, hell, he looked like he had aged five years in the last year. Dark circles beneath his eyes accented the fine lines, and his skin now looked sallow. More than likely, he had slept in the office the night before...and the night before that.

"Why don't you have a seat?" Agent Tsu, his present supervisor, said. "We have a situation."

TJ got the itch on the back of his neck that told him trouble was just around the corner.

"And that would be?" he asked, as he took the other seat in front of the big screen.

"Seems like someone at Task Force Hawaii has been naughty," Remington said. "There has been some...breaches of security in the last few months. Leads all the way back to their people."

"What kind of breaches?"

"Nothing *that* big, until this past weekend. Seems someone was trying to access security codes to find operative names," Remington said. "We caught it on time and we informed the operatives."

"Location?" he asked.

"Far East."

That didn't sound good. Not good at all. Remington was being evasive, and that always meant he wanted TJ to do something that might not be kosher with the bosses—or TJ for that matter.

"So, you want me to question them?" he asked.

"No," Tsu said. "We want you to be the liaison to TFH. They've been asking for one for months. This gives you the perfect cover."

TJ glanced at the screen, then back to Tsu.

"One of the agreements of me taking this job was not to go undercover. Not after the last job."

"It won't be anything dangerous. In fact, we just want background. But, it is the first lead we've had on Foley in over a year."

Ice danced over his nerve endings. Then, anticipation surged before he could control it.

"And you want me to put myself out there again."

He'd requested the job in Hawaii. After the mess of Remington's investigation, TJ had pressed to escape the political minefield of DC. All of the FBI was political, but there it was insane. He wanted to work in his office again, no more undercover. He might carry a sidearm, but he didn't want to use it on a daily basis. He'd had enough of that last year.

"I wouldn't ask if we didn't need this. But we haven't been able to get a hit on Foley until now. The fact that he appeared in your backyard is a good thing. Or, at least using someone in your backyard."

Foley liked to do that. He would find a woman with expertise, or a young man who was looking for a father figure. They would do all the work, break all the laws, and Foley would disappear. Their thank you for the job was usually a bullet to the back of the head—or a lifetime in prison.

"You're considered the expert on him," TJ said.

"True, but it would be best if I don't pop up there and cause a ruckus. You know if I do, he might disappear again," Remington said.

"This way, you can at least get inside the building," Tsu said. "They tend to keep to themselves unless it is required otherwise."

"So we, as a federal agency, are going to play patty cake to try to find something out?"

It sounded like a shit job all the way around. Sure, he might find a lead on Foley, but they wouldn't let him follow it. He would be ordered to hand it off to Remington.

"You know we have the authority to just question their people."

"Yes, but if you do that, you might scare off Foley," Remington said.

TJ heard the unwavering tone and knew he was definitely screwed. If he didn't go along, they would order him to do it. Then, he would either have to comply or get written up for insubordination and asked to hand in his badge.

"Who's the target?" he asked.

Tsu handed him a file. He opened it and found the picture of a stunning woman. Brown skin, sea-green eyes, and a thousand-watt smile.

"This is my target?" he asked as he tore his attention away from the picture. "She looks like a sorority girl."

"Don't be so fooled," Tsu said. "I've been to a few of her lectures. She regularly gets asked to write articles and, on top of that, the University of Hawaii has been after her to teach a class. She's sharp as a tack."

"She also has a record," Remington said.

That definitely caught his attention. "She has a record? How is she working at TFH?" TJ asked.

"She was a juvenile. Broke into the school to change grades."

"Sure, every hacker thinks of doing that at one time or another," TJ said. In fact, TJ's three brothers had bugged him often once they reached the age to understand their brother's abilities.

"Not hers. Woman had straight A's through high school."

"But she broke in to change her grades?"

"Yeah. Doesn't say why since it was juvenile, and apparently her father's family has a lot of pull in the town, so the charges were dropped. Then she went to University of Georgia. Dropped out her junior year."

"Dropped out?"

There was a beat of silence. "Happens sometimes, you know that with computer geeks."

"But this says she is a forensics tech."

"Yes, and she is very good at her job. She can handle all of that and hack like a damned expert. She wrote a few papers, and they got noticed by several agencies. We tried to recruit her—as did the NSA—but the CIA snapped her up before we could. She worked there for a while before she headed off to a few other places before landing in Hawaii. Seems to be settling in since she bought an apartment."

The itch was getting worse. Damn, this was going to be

beyond a shit assignment. "Great. She's going to smell this a mile away."

"What I need you to do is just be the liaison," Tsu said. "It will be a few days, tops."

"And then I just disappear? That's going to go over well."

"They've been screaming for a liaison for months. It won't raise any flags."

He studied Tsu. "So, I'm the lamb to the slaughter, is that it?"

He shrugged. "In a way. I couldn't get a designation for someone to work with them until now."

"Until you think one of them broke several federal laws and is working with a criminal, who not only has been fucking us over for three years, but likes to profit off the deaths of our agents. Gotta love the FBI."

"I'm using it the best I can," Tsu said. "If nothing comes of the investigation, you can keep working with them. We've needed someone over there for more than a year, but the Bureau wasn't happy when Hawaii decided to form a task force like this."

Of course they weren't. The FBI thought they ran the entire country and everyone should bow to their power. It worked sometimes, but even in the few months TJ had been living in Hawaii, he'd learned you couldn't force Hawaiians to do what they didn't want to. It was one of the things he loved about living there. They were the epitome of dancing to the beat of their own drum.

"So, instead of working with them, and taking some of the load off us, the Bureau decided to be assholes and not give them a liaison?"

"Until now. And, we can justify it now that you'll have the job," Tsu said.

"Doesn't really matter in the end," Remington said.

"Why not?" TJ asked.

"If their forensics tech is working for a cyber-criminal like Foley, then I doubt TFH will survive."

And TJ was going to be the lucky bastard who got to rip it apart.

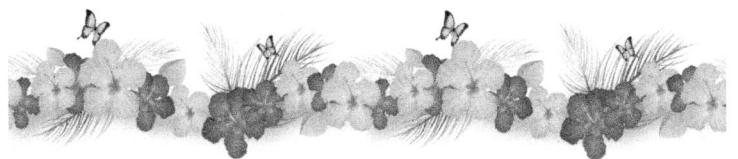

Chapter Two

Monday morning arrived too early for Charity. It started with her alarm not going off. Or, maybe she turned it off in her sleep. She didn't remember. Rushing in the morning was never a good thing, and she did it more than she liked to admit. Later than usual, she didn't even have time to jump in the shower.

She grabbed her favorite black skirt with white polka dots and stepped into it. Why did they have Monday mornings anyway? They all sucked. Sucked a lot. No one wanted to be there and if they got a case on a Monday it was an omen. It was going to be a crappy case that would give Del what she called his "aneurism" face.

Charity hurried into her bathroom and checked out her outfit. It was one of her favorites, and always left her feeling powerful. The knit white shirt hugged her curves and paired nicely with the skirt. As she applied her lipstick, she thought about the weekend. It had been fantastic. Still, spending time with Drew and his family always left her feeling a little homesick.

With a sigh, she capped the lipstick, and headed back into her bedroom. She grabbed a white scarf and walked out into the living room.

Drew was sitting on the couch watching TV. She knew that he hadn't slept much the night before. While a lot of people in the midst of depression might sleep a lot, Drew did the opposite. She heard him walking the apartment at all hours of the night. They didn't speak of it—not yet. She was easing into it. She knew he was restless and that was good. He needed another week or two, then she would push more. It was all a delicate process to get Drew back on his feet.

"You're going to be late," Drew said, without looking at her.

She glanced at him. He was still staring at the TV.

"It's only 8 o'clock, and remember, I live closer than I did before."

He rolled his eyes and picked up Luke, her male cat, as she walked into the kitchen. She knew he hadn't eaten breakfast, and would avoid eating for awhile. Pushing those thoughts aside, she grabbed an energy bar. She snatched up her purse and tossed the bar at Drew, who caught it without looking.

"Good reflexes, slick," she said. "Just make sure you eat it."

Jess came sauntering in, unhappy with the situation. Both her cats had decided they owned Drew, and did not like when the other got attention.

"Why don't you come by for lunch?" she asked, as she wrapped the scarf around her head and tied it at the base of her neck.

"I'll let you know."

Constant Craving

She knew it was a lie. He wasn't going to come into work, hadn't since the shooting. Six months earlier, he'd almost died, and Drew still hadn't worked through the issues. Of course, the fact that his brief romance with Cat Kalakau had hit the skids after the shooting did nothing to help things. Work and romance rarely worked, even though it had seemed to for a couple others on the team.

"You know you can call me any time. Seems we have nothing going on at work at the moment."

Drew shrugged. "The moment you think you have nothing to do, everything will explode in your face."

"You are just a little ray of sunshine."

He gave her a smile that had nothing to do with humor. "Just being a truth teller."

"Well, then you might want to think about helping Elle out."

Drew was Elle's assistant in the ME office for TFH, or he had been. She was sick of using that phrase in her head about him. Knowing that starting an argument right now was the worst way to start off a Monday, she brushed it aside.

"Remember, call me," she said as she grabbed her coffee.

He waved a hand in her direction. She wanted to throw something at him, but there was a good chance her own cats would attack her. And, more than likely, Drew wouldn't even notice it. Shaking her head, she decided concentrating on getting to work was more than enough for her to handle at the moment.

TJ fought the need to pull on his collar. He hated deception. It made no sense that he was good at undercover work since he loathed to lie, but he apparently had a knack for it. That's why he found himself standing in front of the captain for Task Force Hawaii Monday morning.

"So, the FBI decided to stop dicking us around?" Captain Delano said.

TJ smiled. "Now, I wouldn't go *that* far."

Delano chuckled. "Please, sit down. Makes me feel like I'm in the Army again with you standing there."

TJ did as Delano asked. In the few minutes he had spent in Delano's presence, TJ discovered that he liked him. Former military, no nonsense, and blunt to a fault. TJ would take that over slick and smooth talking any day. He liked to know where he stood with a person. There was no doubt in TJ's mind that a person would know exactly how Delano felt about him. He liked someone or he hated them. Delano would probably have no gray areas in his life.

"We aren't that formal here, so you might not like dealing with us much."

"I've heard that about you."

"I like a man who speaks his mind."

Delano leaned back, and the casual observer would look at him and think he was relaxing. TJ knew better. The former Army officer's gaze moved over TJ, and he had to fight the need to fidget. It was an odd feeling, one he rarely got; except when his father was studying him. Delano didn't miss anything with that clear gaze.

"You're probably the first public official that would," TJ said.

"I value honesty above blind devotion. Don't get me

wrong. I don't like people to buck orders, but I do like to have open communications. Our team thrives on it. So, the fact that you are honest means we'll deal well with each other. Most of the office will be gathering for a meeting in a few minutes, so it will be easiest to introduce you to them."

"Most? Not all?"

"Well, Cat is on vacation over on Maui. Then we have one out due to injury. Oh, and there is always a good chance Charity will be late. She lives the closest, but the woman is hardly ever on time."

"And you put up with that because?"

"First, she's only late by five minutes most of the time. If you have lived here for any amount of time, you know everything runs late in Hawaii. Second, she's a first rate forensic tech who rarely asks for overtime pay. We were lucky to nab her here for the salary we offered. When you meet her you'll understand."

He didn't need to meet her to understand. He had spent the weekend working on installing his kitchen cabinets and reading up on Charity Edwards. She not only had a first rate mind when it came to computers, but some of her forensic testing had been adopted by not only the HPD, but also the FBI. It was her ability to think outside the box that had garnered her the most success.

That's what worried TJ the most. A person with no real rules of engagement when it came to testing often would take chances in other parts of her life—including getting tangled up with Foley. It would be out of character, but he wasn't sure he could pin down her.

"What might help is if you give me an explanation of how you handle a case with the team."

Delano nodded. "We don't have partners on the team."

"Then how do you work a case?"

"We structured the team to work together at all times. The FBI has files on all of us, so you can get an idea that we all have different strengths."

"Group management?"

"No." The denial was quick enough to tell TJ that Delano didn't have a problem with the question. "I'm in charge, but I do believe that our structure allows us to solve cases that might give other departments issues."

"I don't know how that would work in the real world."

"First, we are the real world."

"Noted," TJ said, acknowledging he had hit a nerve.

"Working a case within HPD is hard. In any department. My team isn't graded on their amount of collars. We all get credit. So, they aren't trying to steal cases from each other. It wouldn't work in a bigger department. A small department like ours has our advantages, but we do have our limits. We aren't here for normal policing. We normally take on one case at a time, all of working the same issue. When they throw the case at us, it is either a hot case, crosses state and federal lines, or it is a FUBAR that no one wants. We have to work differently to succeed."

TJ nodded. "Makes sense."

And it did. They had a pretty high success rate their first eighteen months in existence."

Delano studied him. "You like doing everything by the book?"

"Yeah, for the most part."

"Oh, you are going to have fun with us."

Constant Craving

Charity walked into TFH headquarters and found everyone hanging out in the conference area, which was about normal since they had an early morning meeting. This morning though, there was something different.

"Where's the boss?" she asked.

Emma, Del's wife, rubbed her hand over her rounded belly and nodded toward Del's office door. She was in the last six weeks of her pregnancy. "Looks like we finally have an FBI liaison."

Charity turned towards the door, and immediately lost almost every thought in her brain. Good lord, the man walking beside Del was gorgeous. He was tall, about the same height as Del, who was well over six feet. But, he wasn't bulky like Del. He had more of what they called a swimmer's build. Long and lean. He had slightly wavy dirty blond hair. She wanted to slip her fingers through his thick locks. He had a tan, not uncommon in Hawaii, but it looked natural on him. The golden tone to his skin brought out his light gray eyes. He dressed in a suit and a tie that made him stand out in Hawaii. Even the mayor of Honolulu didn't wear a tie. Usually, she would dismiss him because of that, but there was something about him. He definitely knew how to wear a suit.

"Oh, great, everyone is here," Del said.

"Drew is still not here and Cat's on leave," Emma said. Emma Delano was a genius, who took almost every statement literally.

Del shook his head. "I mean all of us who are active at the moment."

She shrugged and said nothing. From the disinterest she

was showing, Charity knew Emma had something else on her mind. Her brain was always working on something.

"This is Agent TJ Callahan of the FBI. He's our new liaison with the feds, so make nice with him."

Charity glanced at the agent in question to see if he was irritated. From the way his mouth twitched, Charity was guessing he wasn't.

"This is the team. You can learn all their names as they go along."

Adam stepped forward with a smile. As second-in-command, he was a formidable man, well over six feet tall, a shiny bald head, and his Hawaiian and Polynesian ancestry stamped on his pretty face. His size made him intimidating, but Charity knew the fierce look hid a softer side.

"Hey, Hammer," he said, shaking the agent's hand. "So, I see they stuck you with this job."

"What can I say? The boss loves me."

"I didn't know you knew Adam," Del said.

"We met during that first responders conference year before last," Agent Callahan said. "I had just moved to the island, and you were with the HPD then, right?"

"Yeah. Moved over here a few months later. I can show you around TFH if you want."

"Sounds good, but truth is, I'm not going to be haunting the hallways."

"Sure," Emma said, rubbing her rounded tummy. "That's what Carino from HPD said, and he is over here all the time."

"He says we have better food," Marcus said.

"We do," Emma said. "As long as he knows not to spread

the word around. I am *not* sharing any cocoa puffs with those losers."

"Emma, I've asked you not to call them losers," Del said. Since becoming pregnant, Emma had become a little mercenary about food, especially her favorite treat.

"They come in here and take one of my cocoa puffs, they won't be losers. They'll be dead."

Del shook his head and apparently decided to ignore that comment. "So, why don't I introduce you to the team."

Del's phone went off before he could begin, and he looked at the screen. The grimace meant it was someone he did not want to talk to.

"It's the mayor. Adam, can you handle this?"

"I was born for the job," Adam said.

"Thanks. I'll catch you later, Callahan. Good to have you on board."

He clicked on his phone as he headed to his office for privacy.

Adam smiled. "So, you know me, which is the most important person to know."

"I bet your mother tells you that," Marcus said.

"Of course she does. She's a smart woman." He motioned toward Emma. "This is Emma Delano, she's one of our contractors."

"Hey. Do you like cocoa puffs?"

TJ blinked, trying to follow the conversation. Most people looked like that the first time they had a conversation with Emma. "The cereal or the pastry from Liliha's?"

Emma rolled her eyes. "The pastries."

"I do."

"You have to put in an order ahead of time if I go."

TJ didn't say anything but nodded.

"This is Floyd," he said, waving his hand to Marcus.

TJ narrowed his gaze. "DC police?"

Marcus smiled. "You remember."

He nodded. "Seems we all are trying to escape the next snowmaggeden."

"The tall goofy looking one back there is McGregor. Dr. Elle Middleton is standing beside him. Then, this is our Charity."

"*Our* Charity?" she asked.

"Yeah," Adam said. "You're ours, and no other agency gets you. We just like them to know that."

"Great. Now I know how you really feel about me." She turned and smiled at the agent, who was staring at her with a dazed expression on his face. "It's nice to meet you."

He pulled himself together and nodded. "Likewise." Then he glanced around. "I had another name on the list. Drew Franklin."

"He's recovering."

TJ raised his eyebrows at that, but before he could ask them anything about it, Adam took over. "Why don't I show you around the place?"

"What about the meeting?" Charity asked.

"Del said we would reschedule for one," Adam said.

"Oh, good. I'm in the mood for some cocoa puffs from Liliha Bakery. Any takers?" Emma asked.

Everyone but the agent raised their hands.

"Great."

She waved at Del before leaving the room.

"Come on, Callahan. I'll show you all our offices."

"Mine's locked," Charity said. "I haven't had time to get down there."

"We'll save you for last."

"Of course you will. I am the best." She waited until they were gone.

"Be still my little Georgia heart. That is one big hunk of man meat."

"And from Texas," Floyd said.

"Yeah?"

He nodded. "I remember he's's a big Dallas Cowboy fan."

"Hmm, I do like Texan men."

"He's a Fed," Floyd said, the tone of his voice telling her exactly how he felt about feds. Most of the team had a bad view of the feds for some reason or another, but since Charity had been one, they didn't really bother her.

"And?"

He shrugged his massive shoulders. Another big guy, former Capitol Police from DC. He was a quiet hulk of a man, who knew his way around a firearm and was considered an expert on terrorism. "I had to work with them when I was in DC, and it wasn't always fun."

"Why?"

"He's a *by the book* kind of guy, and he doesn't always play well with others."

She looked at Marcus. "A dark side?"

He shook his head. "No. He's a little like Emma. Quiet, kind of keeps to himself. I think it is a computer nerd thing.

"Hey, I'm a computer nerd."

"You are not your average nerd. You are very unique."

She smiled. "You definitely know how to talk pretty. I

would assume you were from the South if I didn't know better."

He shook his head. "Just know that Hammer doesn't always want to work with other people, and he has no problem letting them know."

"I'm not planning on working *with* him."

On him, yeah, but with him, probably not. There were all kinds of things she wanted to do to him, and it started with getting him naked as soon as possible.

Before Floyd could respond, Del stepped out into the conference area. The frown he was sporting told Charity that the phone call hadn't been fun. He glanced around the conference room. "Where did Emma go?"

"She wanted some cocoa puffs," Charity said.

Del rolled his eyes. "I should buy stock in the bakery. They are going to bankrupt me by the time that baby gets here. I'm heading over to HPD. The mayor wants me to talk shop about security for an upcoming conference. I should be back in time for the meeting."

With that, he headed out the door, and she sat down at the table.

"Aren't you supposed to go downstairs and get ready?" Marcus asked.

She shrugged. "You know how longwinded Adam can be. It'll take him over an hour to make it to my lab."

Marcus smiled. "That's true. How's Drew?"

She shrugged. "Some days are good. He did a little better when I dragged him to my place, but now I can't seem to get him off my couch. I did get him out this weekend to see his family. He spends more time with Luke and Jess than anyone else."

He shook his head. "That's not good. No man should spend most of his days with cats."

"I agree, but other than dragging him to see his family, I can't get him out of there. I thought being in Honolulu would get him to the beach. You know that boy likes to surf."

"I take it Cat hasn't been by?"

She shook her head. "I just want to slap her, but then, there is a good chance she would break my face."

"Or shoot you."

"There is that, although, I'm an expert shot. I'm not that good with the hand-to-hand combat."

"That's because you grew up an only child. You learn plenty of combat if you come from a big family."

She chuckled. Marcus came from a family with five kids, all boys.

"Tell you what. Why don't I get Adam and Graeme—and the boss if we can spring him for a night—and take Drew out? We need a guy's night."

"So, no luck with Tamilya, huh?"

Tamilya Lowe was former FBI, and now worked in Hawaii for a private security firm. It was well known that Marcus had been hung up on her forever.

"The woman is playing hard to get."

"And this is something new?"

"Yes. When we dated in DC, she definitely didn't play hard to get."

That bit of information caught her attention. "So, you dated when she was at the FBI?"

For a second, he said nothing. Marcus was like that. He was quiet and often took in everything before making a comment. It was hard to relate to him sometimes because

Charity rarely thought before she spoke. But, the fact that he'd let out the detail that he'd dated Tamilya in the past meant that he was really messed up about her.

"Did you say you wanted help with Drew?"

Her need for gossip warred with her need to help one of her best friends. Drew didn't need to spend all his days hanging around an apartment like a sad version of a brooding loner. Charity understood that if she didn't help him move on from the incident, that there was a good chance he'd quit his job at TFH—he didn't need it anyway—and slip away. It was something that all of them were worried about on some level.

She smiled. "Tamilya who?"

"See that you keep it that way."

She rose from her seat, grabbing her purse. "I better get down to my lab before the hunk from Texas shows up."

Chapter Three

TJ watched the elevator door close and almost sighed with relief. He had done his time in other departments, and his undercover assignment had been dicey-especially the last one. He still got an uneasy stomach in the morgue, especially when people were eating. Elle was competent and very sweet, and she ate cocoa puffs while surrounded by bins of dead people. It was enough to make him want to hurl. It was a little unmanning.

"I never get used to it," Adam said, leaning forward to hit the button.

TJ glanced at him. "Yeah."

"I mean, eating with all those dead people in there."

Adam shuddered dramatically. TJ liked the former HPD officer, and found him to be a straight shooter. At the moment, he was finding it hard to believe anyone in the organization would do something illegal. In the process of an investigation, TJ was pretty sure the team might step over the line. For personal gain...he just wasn't seeing it.

"It's definitely weird. There was an ME in DC who would eat a pastrami sandwich while cutting open a body."

"I think I just threw up in my mouth a little bit."

TJ smiled. "Where to next?"

"The forensics lab."

"And that's Charity's domain?"

Adam gave him a strange look. "Yeah, that's what she calls it. And believe me, you don't want to mess with her domain. Floyd got caught playing around on one of her computers once. It wasn't pretty."

"Yeah, most techs are territorial. And the one person you're missing?"

Adam's humor faded, and a shadow moved over his expression. "That would be Drew. If you were here a few months ago, you heard about the shooting."

Of course he had, as well as having all the internal memos to help him get a feel of the team. But it was always better to let people talk.

"Oh, yeah."

Adam nodded. "Drew was clinically dead at least once after they got him to Tripler, but he pulled through."

And the team still hadn't recovered from the looks of it. Of course, if Franklin hadn't moved on, they might have issues. "When is he expected back at work?"

"Soon, hopefully. Charity's working on him."

That caught TJ's attention. "Charity?"

"Yeah. He's staying with her while he recuperates."

That information had not been included in the report, so there is a good chance it had just happened. It brought about another whole list of concerns.

"Are they an item?"

"Naw, just friends. She's trying to help him recuperate, and being with family is comforting, and sometimes overbearing. So, Charity asked him to move in with her for awhile."

TJ had no time to respond, as the doors opened and they were thrown into chaos. Tim McGraw's voice blared, as bright light from a bank of windows to the right illuminated every possible spot. TJ blinked trying to get his eyes to focus.

"Good God, Charity," Adam said. "Turn that crap down."

She turned with a gasp, but it blossomed into a grin. Damn, the woman had a great smile. It wasn't one of those cool professional smiles. Happiness filled her expression and her eyes lit up. It was the kind of smile every man wanted to see when he arrived home.

Whoa, dial it back, Callahan.

"You come to my lab, you deal with Tim."

Adam scrubbed a hand over his bald head. "Last week it was Adam Levine."

"Come on, Adam. Every week is Adam Levine week."

Adam shook his head. "You met Agent Callahan earlier."

"Of course," she said, directing that smile in his direction.

Again, the slow beat of arousal thrummed through his blood. He had expected some attraction, as she was a beautiful woman. He didn't know a heterosexual man who wouldn't be attracted to her. Average height, definitely on the curvy side, she dressed as if she were a movie queen from the fifties. It added to the attraction a bit. There was something about a woman in three inch heels and a swing to her step that mesmerized him. His fingers itched to touch to see just out warm her light brown flesh was. This was not good. She was his assignment, and being attracted to her was not going to help in the investigation.

"Nice set up."

Great. That was cool, Callahan. Way to sound like a genius.

She nodded. "The best on the island. HPD is so jealous of my lab. I'm sure the feds would be too, if they ever got a gander at it. You're the first one I've had in here."

It was odd that no feds had been in to see the lab. He had a feeling TFH liked being left on their own. Then, he really looked around and discovered that she definitely had a top quality lab. He knew most of the equipment by sight. Computer forensics was more his forte, but it was easy to see that most of it was less than a year old. It made sense because TFH hadn't been around that long, but it was still damned remarkable.

"Impressive, although, I'm wondering how you got the money from state. It's hard to get money out of the federal government, but I know state governments have been strapped the last few years."

Charity shrugged. "Del took care of it. I believe it was through some grants."

"Resourceful."

"It helps he had time dealing with the federal government when he was in the Army. Plus, Adam knows a few people, doncha?"

Adam smiled. "I know too many people. It's a hazard of being born and raised on Oahu. Everyone knows everyone else."

"Del says that's the only reason he's keeping you around."

Adam shook his head, but before he could respond, his

phone when off. He read the text message and his humor dissolved. "Hey, I have an issue I have to take care of. Can you handle TJ?"

For a moment, the question hung in the air between them. Charity's mouth twitched, and there was a glint in her eyes, but she didn't say anything.

Oblivious to the tension, Adam said, "Charity?"

She tore her gaze from TJ to look at Adam. "Yeah, sure."

"Catch you later, Hammer. I'm sure the boss would like to talk to you again if he's back."

Before TJ could say anything, Adam hurried out leaving them alone.

"That call was not work related," Charity said with a shake of her head.

"Oh?"

Charity dismissed him with another shake of her head. "Just an old case that's very personal for him."

"But you just said that it wasn't work related."

"She isn't."

He saw the look on her face and knew not to push. He wouldn't be able to gain her trust if he pushed too hard.

"What is it you need to know about my lab? About my role at TFH?"

And right then and there, he couldn't think of anything. His mind was blank as he watched her saunter into her office. God, the woman knew how to walk. Damn, he knew when he saw her pic, it was going to be tough. Throw in that megawatt smile and Southern twang, and there was a good chance he would walk around without most of his blood in his brain.

She turned back to look at him. "Are you coming?"

Someone was playing a huge joke on him. That was all he could think of. It had to be a sadistic fuck too. To pick out a woman who fit his idea of an ideal woman. She was curvy, with a sassy little walk that he was sure drew a lot of attention. On top of that, she was smart. There was no way she could have worked at the CIA or TFH and been stupid.

"Sure," he said, finally following her into the office. Like the rest of the area, it seemed to be jam-packed with junk, but he knew better. He could see the patterns of organization. Pictures of what he expected was her family filled the credenza behind the desk. Her geekiness was on display here. Bobble heads of the Avengers, a few Pokémon figurines, but front and center was the Flash. A poster and a rather large figurine sat in the middle of the credenza.

"Wow."

She sat down behind her desk. "You like?"

"What's not to like? My parents would kill for some of this."

"Oh?"

He nodded. "Dad's a retired Texas Ranger, but they now own and operate the biggest comic book store in South Texas."

"Cool."

"The Flash figurine?"

She smiled. "Custom made. Nothing too good for my man Barry."

"So you consider yourself a DC kind of woman?"

"No, I'm more of a fan of Marvel; although, I love all things superhero. But Flash, well, he has my job. So, I know he's a badass."

He hadn't really thought about it that way. "True."

"So, what is your job?"

"I handle computer crimes."

Her eyes lit up with interest. "Cyber crimes? Oh, I miss that. I do a little of that here, but only if it pertains to one of our cases."

He heard it—that hacker excitement. TJ had always said that most people working cyber crimes were just hackers who had the right to invade privacy. They did it behind a badge, but they shared the same need to pry into the dark places of the Internet. "So you handle all the forensics?"

"Yes. We have most everything we need here. Del was worried that we would be on the bottom of the pile for HPD. They have enough to worry about anyway. If they can't do it, we have to send it to the mainland, and with the cases we take, that isn't really feasible. They usually have high visibility, meaning that the press is usually breathing down Del's neck."

"Sounds great, but still, impressive that he got all of that equipment here."

She nodded. "That's Del, though. He's a good guy. And he knows how to work things. And, like I said, if he doesn't, Adam does."

He looked around and said nothing else. He was done with the tour, and he should just go back upstairs and see if Delano was back, but he didn't want to leave. It had nothing to do with the job, although it should have. He should want to spend a little more time with unfettered access in her lab and office.

"Anything else?"

He shook his head. "Not really." He glanced at his watch. "Do you have time to grab a coffee?"

She blinked, and he felt something shift beneath him. Why the hell had he asked her out for coffee? He shouldn't have done that. This was work, and, yes, he needed to investigate her, but he had planned on asking the team out so he could get the feel of the dynamics.

"Not really. I have to go over testimony with the DA today for a case that is coming up next week."

He nodded, relieved and disappointed at the same time.

She hesitated, then asked, "How about dinner?"

He should say no. This was too personal and exactly what had happened the last time, but he couldn't find the nerve. "Sure. When?"

"Tonight."

It was there, on the tip of his tongue to say no. He needed to call Remington and give him his first impressions and do a little more research on the team, especially Charity. But he couldn't. For the first time in a long time, he was definitely interested in spending more time with a woman.

"Tonight is fine."

"Great. How does seven sound?"

"Seven is fantastic."

"If you give me your number, I can send you my deets."

He rattled off the number, and she entered it in her cell.

"Well, I guess I should go upstairs."

"Del should be back by now. He hates meetings in general, and especially things like this with the mayor."

"I'll see you tonight."

She gave him that smile and his heart did a little dance. Damn.

"Sounds good."

As he walked to the elevator, he chastised himself. He

needed to keep it impersonal, and he should cancel the date, right then. Or even by text later, but he knew better. He had to keep relations good between him and the team during the investigation.

Adam stepped off the elevator on the floor where the holding cells for HPD were. He had been making too many trips here lately, he thought.

He approached the desk as Jason Kalua shook his head. The older officer had trained Adam years ago. Kalua had been thirty pounds lighter and had a lot more hair in those days, but he was a solid cop.

"We're not going to be able to keep calling you, Lee. At some point, she's going to have to face the music."

Adam sighed and scrubbed a hand over his scalp. "I understand. I'm trying."

Kalua nodded. "I know, and that's why we've been giving her a break, but this time, we caught her in her car."

"Her car?"

"Not driving, but just sitting there. Dozing actually. But the keys were in the ignition."

"Okay."

He turned to walk away, but Kalua stopped him. "Get her in a program, *bra*. I know she has issues, and that's why we let her off all the time, but if she's driving next time, she could kill herself or someone else."

"I know. I'm working on it."

"She's in five."

Adam nodded and made his way down the corridor to her

cell. He found her laying on the cot. This was not the Jin Phillips he had met two years ago. She had been bright and flirty, so full of life. A week in hell had transformed her into a woman he didn't even recognize.

He sighed. She looked so peaceful, but he knew better. He knew the memories that haunted her, that drinking was her way to forget.

The guard unlocked the door, and Adam approached her quietly.

He watched her sleep for a few moments. He hated to wake her up, but he had to get her out of there. The monsters she had worked with in the news industry would love to find out about this. They would relish exposing her fall from disgrace, the bastards.

He squatted down. "Jin."

She frowned and he smiled. It was the sweetest little frown.

"Hey, Jin, wake up, baby," he said raising his voice a bit.

Her eyes opened slowly, a small smile replacing the frown. Then, she screamed. He jerked back and almost fell over.

She blinked as she sat up. "Adam? What are you doing here?"

Then, she looked around. Her shoulders sagged. "Damn."

"Yeah," Adam said, rising back up. "They found you in your car."

She rubbed her face with one hand. "I don't remember."

"Yeah, I get that. What the hell were you thinking?"

He hadn't meant to question her. He knew that never ended well.

Constant Craving

She narrowed her eyes at him. "I don't think it's any of your damned business."

He wanted to argue, but he didn't. He pushed the irritation and anger aside and held out his hand. She looked at it, then stood up on her own.

"I'll take you back to Aiea."

She shook her head. "Just take me to my car."

"Jin."

"No, Adam. Just take me to my car."

He wanted to yell, to scream at her for being this way, but he couldn't. He had no right, especially since he still felt responsible for the ordeal she had been through. Instead, he nodded and followed her out of the cell. He knew if something didn't happen soon, she was going to hurt herself or someone else. Each time he got a message about her, he had thought it would be that they found her body.

But right now, all he did was follow her onto the elevator.

By the time TJ made it back to the office, he had, thankfully, missed the Monday meeting. The traffic had been a bitch, especially since it wasn't rush hour, but that was Oahu. Still, he couldn't complain since he hated meetings. Before joining the FBI, he had spent a lot of his time alone. Being the geek of his family, he had often fought for alone time in a big family like his. With three brothers, he rarely got his wish, but his mother had understood. She had made sure he had some privacy.

Damn, he had meant to call her this weekend and forgot. Working on the rehab of his house was taking up all his free time. Throw in a bitch of an assignment and he had forgotten. There would be hell to pay, that was for sure.

He stepped into his office, shutting the door behind him just as his cell rang. Damn. Remington.

TJ knew better than to ignore him, and answered the call.

"So, how did today go?"

Of course he knew TJ had gone in. There wasn't much Remington didn't know when he was working a job.

"Yeah. Just got back."

"So, thoughts?"

As he made his way over to his desk, he answered. "Definitely a close knit group."

"They've been operating less than two years, correct?"

"Yeah, but you can see the camaraderie within the group. A lot of them are transplants too with no family here."

"And that makes it easier to build a strong office relationship. I can see that. So what about Charity Edwards?"

What about her? She knocked his socks off when she smiled at him and he wanted to see her naked was all he could think of.

"Seems sweet, with all that Southern charm. But, she's tough."

"She'd have to be to deal with the CIA. What I want to know is if you think she could be the hacker?"

No. It was a gut instinct that had served him well, but he suppressed it. Remington didn't want to hear that. He wanted facts.

"I'm leaning on the side of no, but I'll find out more tonight."

"Oh?"

"She asked me out to dinner tonight. I figured it would be

a good idea. Being away from the office might loosen her up a bit."

"Good. Though, I want you to remember this is a job. Don't get too involved with her."

Of course Remington would say that. The last job they had worked on had left one woman dead and TJ near death because he'd thought she might be innocent or, at the very least, ready to turn on Foley.

"Right. You got it."

"Check in tomorrow and let me know how it goes tonight."

"Sure."

Remington hung up without saying goodbye. TJ stood and went to the window. He could barely see the ocean from his office on the third floor, but he knew it was there. He had wanted to live closer to work, but when he had found his way to Waimanalo one weekend, he had fallen in love. Then, he'd found a rundown former crack house and fell in love once again. He liked how quiet it was, how there were more locals than tourists, and he couldn't beat the view from the hill he lived on.

With a sigh, he stepped away from the window. He needed to do a little more background work on Charity before their date. He still felt a little guilty about it, but reminded himself she had been the one to ask. It was a copout and he knew it, but the sooner he got to the bottom of this mess, the sooner he could clear his conscious. And if there was a tiny part of him that wanted it to be more than just part of the investigation, then he pushed it away. He couldn't take a chance and lose to Foley again.

Chapter Four

Charity made it back to TFH headquarters well after lunch. With no lunch and waited time, she had moved from hungry to hangry in the last half hour. She didn't mind meetings with the DA. She saw them as tests, and one of the many things Charity was good at was tests. Not only did she excel at them, she truly enjoyed the preparation. But this ADA hadn't been prepared and had expected her to just sit there while he worked on getting prepared. It was annoying.

She set her purse down just as Elle came through her door.

"Hey, you're finally back."

"Yeah. Have you dealt with ADA Deason yet?" she asked, grabbing an apple and some water out of her little fridge.

Elle nodded and frowned. "Yes. He's never ready and always blames it on me."

"Great. I wish I had known about that."

"He did make the mistake of not being ready for Emma one time."

Charity rolled her eyes, as she bit into her apple. Emma was sweet, but she was not patient. She also believed everyone else worked on her schedule. Charity could only imagine what Emma had done to the ADA.

"Do you need something?"

Elle shook her head. "Just...I hate to admit, I'm bored. Without Drew here and no cases, I'm stuck in the morgue all by myself."

"I thought Graeme was keeping you company down there."

The TFH team member and the doctor had been living together for a few months. With Drew out of commission, Graeme had been working from his desk when he wasn't needed elsewhere.

Elle nodded. "But he had a meeting to attend. And he's not happy with me right now."

"Oh, no. No trouble in paradise, I hope," she said as she opened an email from her mentor at the CIA.

Elle shook her head. "He's just being pigheaded."

Charity laughed. "Darlin', you knew that before you got together with him."

"Yeah, and I find it cute sometimes."

"But not now."

Elle shook her head, but Charity's attention locked on the message.

Charity,

Just wanted to give you a heads up. There is chatter about Foley in your region of the world. Be extra careful.

Dr. Summers

"What?" Elle asked.

Charity looked at her friend. "Sorry. Just a report from an old boss. Dr. Summers says there is chatter about a nasty hacker."

"Oh?"

"Yeah. He's what you and Graeme would call a wanker of the first order."

"That bad?"

"The FBI almost caught him once. See, the dude uses other people to hack. Mostly women, romances them, then leaves them to take the rap while he runs away with money."

"What a wanker."

"See?"

Elle smiled. "You don't know him?"

Charity shook her head. "Let's just say, I'm not someone who would fit his profile hit. I have a close family. Most of these women were on their own. They have few family or friends and they rarely date."

"Sad."

"Yeah, and the last incident involved a woman who got killed. Not fun for anyone. And Foley just danced away with the cash again. Worse, no one knows what he looks like, and we don't even know if Foley is his real name."

"Even with all our surveillance video around the world, we haven't caught him?"

Charity shook her head. "I always thought he had some kind of connection to law enforcement, or had hacked into their computers. There are all kinds of rumors that he is in the government, high up. He has access to information that the normal layperson doesn't have available. Well, a non-hacker, at least, wouldn't know."

"Like what?"

Charity shrugged as she closed out her email. "He always seems to know how to avoid cameras. He also knows inside info about agencies that is hard to know unless you work for them."

"That's fun to know."

Charity smiled. "I could ask our new FBI Liaison about it."

Elle settled into the chair in front of Charity's desk. "Whenever we see him again."

"I'm seeing him tonight."

Charity saw that it took more than a second or two for what she said to sink in. "Wait, what?"

"I asked him out on a date. Well, first he asked me to coffee, but I had to go deal with that idiot Deason. So, I asked him to dinner. I couldn't pass up a man like that."

Elle shook her head. "You rarely do when you are attracted."

She knew it wasn't a slam. Elle had never been judgmental. "Lately, it has been tough. Drew is not conducive to dating."

"Oh, I'm sorry, Charity. Do you need me to start bugging him?"

She watched the doctor lean back in her seat and close her eyes. She was pale and looked under the weather. Then, Charity remembered she wasn't feeling well last week either.

"No. I can handle the boy. And that's what I'm calling him now. He is acting like a boy."

Elle's mouth curved, but she said nothing.

"Hey, woman, are you sick?"

Elle opened one eye. "No, just old. Remember, I have ten years on you."

"You are not old."

"Maybe not, but the long days are harder on me than they are on you."

Charity chuckled. "I don't have a giant Scotsman keeping me up at night either."

"There is that."

"Well, I am going to go through the rest of my emails and then I am shutting down."

"Dinner you say?" Elle asked.

"Yeah. You know when a strong strapping Texan walks into my life, and he is seemingly unconnected, I'm going to have a try at him."

"So, that's what gets to you?"

Charity shrugged. "That and he seems to be a geek. Plus, with the computer background, I think we would have a lot in common. It will be nice to have dinner conversation that doesn't involve grunts from a grumpy little boy."

Elle nodded. "Let me know how it goes."

When she was alone, Charity did just as she'd said. She wanted enough time to shower and get ready for her date.

TJ's phone rang as he was about to walk out the door. Damn, his mother.

"Hey, Mom. Kind of busy at the moment."

"You're always busy at work. You can at least stop and chat with your mother for a moment."

His mother had not taken him moving to Hawaii very

well. Hell, she had been pissed when he had left Texas for DC. And she had one other thing she liked to complain to him about.

"So, you called to complain that I don't have a social life?"

"And to make sure you're still alive."

"Aww, you really don't have to do that."

"I do because I am your mother."

"I just meant that the FBI would contact you if I were dead."

"That's not funny."

"I'll make it up to you then."

"How? Are you coming out for a visit?"

"No, but I'm actually on my way out to pick up a date."

There was a beat of silence. "That's good."

"Is there anything else?"

"Well, you could tell me about this date."

"Her name is Charity and I met her today. That's all I am saying. So, unless there is an emergency with y'all, I have to get back to Honolulu."

"Call me this weekend."

"Yes, ma'am."

"You don't fool me, young man. I know that there's something else going on there."

Of course she did. His mother always knew when he and his brothers were shaving the truth. Being married to a Texas Ranger for over thirty-five years had taught her well.

"I'll call."

"Love you."

"Love you back."

He clicked off his phone and slipped into his jeep with a bigger smile than at first. The evening air was thick with the heavy perfume of flowers. In the year he had lived in Hawaii, he still wasn't used to the beauty he experienced on a daily basis.

He started down the hill that led to Kam Highway. He lived in Waimanalo, just a short drive to Honolulu. Hell, everywhere was a short drive to Honolulu on the island. But he liked living in an area that was filled with more locals than transplants.

Wind whipped through his hair as he turned onto Kam Highway. The traffic was moderate, considering it was high tourist season. It wouldn't take him that long to make it to Charity's.

He should have called the date off. Normally, he wouldn't have a problem with it, but the fact that he didn't told him two things. One, he was definitely interested in her outside of work. Two, he had doubts that she was their hacker. After reading through her file, TJ had serious misgivings that Charity was stupid enough to fall for Foley's schemes. She definitely didn't fit the profile for Foley. She had friends, an active social life that made even his brother Luke look like a monk, and a very close family. Foley tended to find loners, people who had dysfunctional relationships and needed support. TJ was also sure that the FBI would never have traced it back to her if it had been her. She was just that damned smart.

Still, he needed information from her, but taking her on a date, that was different. And while he knew he should have canceled, he couldn't seem to bring himself to. He would see where it would go, and maybe he could definitely make sure she was protected no matter what.

Charity looked at herself in the mirror and sighed. She did not have time to change again. She'd tried for casual with jeans, but it hadn't felt right. The sundress she had on was one of her favorites. Bright yellow with a v-cut neckline that showed off her cleavage just enough. It was A-line in design, and fell to just below her knees. She wore a matching belt and a pair of peekaboo shoes in white. Her hair was down.

Her phone buzzed, breaking her out of her study. It was Emma.

"So, whatcha doing?" Emma asked as she munched on something.

"Getting ready for a date."

"Ohhh, who are you going out with?"

"That cute FBI agent. He asked me out."

There was a pause. "Callahan?"

"Yeah. It's been a few weeks since I've had any prospects, because *you know who* doesn't help."

Emma grunted. The sound was rude and funny at the same time. "Del told me the guys are springing him this weekend."

"That will be good."

"Now, back to the fed."

Charity put away the last outfit she had tried on. "You say that as if he is the enemy."

"I don't trust feds."

"You trust me."

"You aren't a fed."

"But I was."

"Not anymore. Now you're ours."

Constant Craving

The common sense tone in Emma's voice made Charity smile. Emma had lost most of her family a decade earlier to the tsunami in Thailand. Charity knew that Emma counted everyone on the team as her family. In fact, she was practically territorial about it.

"Still. And it's just a date."

"Be careful. There is something off about him that bothers me."

She stopped. "What do you mean?"

"Not sure, but I don't like him."

That was odd. Emma didn't like most people at first. She had issues dealing with people, especially one-on-one. Daily interaction with the team had helped her come out of her shell in recent months, but she rarely said things like that.

"Maybe it's the hormones."

Emma snorted. "Could be. I had a bad day, and I cried in front of Del. He didn't know what to do."

Charity couldn't help it. She laughed out loud. The man had been through the ringer during the pregnancy. It started off with sympathy morning sickness, and now he was dealing with an increasingly emotional Emma. Thinking of big, bad Martin Delano bewildered by tears made her heart happy, for both of them.

"Sure, laugh all you want. You can deal with him tomorrow when he's grumpy about it."

"I'll hide in my lab."

"There is that."

The doorbell rang and Charity's heart jumped into her throat. Damn. She hadn't been this nervous about a date in years.

"He's here. I have to go."

"Be good."

"Never." She hung up and hurried out of her bedroom. She heard the male voices before she stepped into the living room.

"Drew Franklin?" TJ asked.

"Yeah," Drew responded. "Latest flavor of the month, I presume?"

"What?"

She was going to kill him. She was going to hurt him first and make him cry, then she would kill him. She didn't care if she counted Drew as one of her best friends in Hawaii and prayed for his recovery just a few months earlier. He needed to die.

When she stepped through the doorway, she found Drew leaning against the door giving TJ a nasty look.

"TJ," she said, shooting what she called her pageant smile in his direction. "I should have known you would be on time."

He glanced over at her, then froze for a second. His gaze traveled down her body then back up before making eye contact. His mouth curved slightly and heat tingled through her blood.

Oh, mama.

"Charity." His Texas twang had deepened over the syllables of her name. "You look great."

Her cats moved in his direction and she cringed. Luke and Jess were always a handful, and they rarely liked strangers. When they ventured out to sniff at one, she knew it could turn out badly.

Luke leaned forward and sniffed at TJ's shoe, as Jess approached more slowly. TJ glanced down, and then slowly lowered his hand so that Jess could sniff at it. Jess hesitated, and she knew that was a bad sign. There was a good chance she would scratch TJ hard enough to draw blood. But, instead, Jess sniffed, then slipped her head under his hand allowing TJ to pet her.

"They like you."

He looked up and shot her a full smile that revealed dimples. Lord have mercy. The man was a killer with that grin.

"They seem nice enough to me."

"It took them a month to get used to Drew here," she said, smirking at her roommate.

"I still have the scratches to prove it, the little bastards."

TJ straightened. "Are you ready to go?"

"Sure." She grabbed her purse, then stepped into her shoes. "Don't wait up, Drew."

"Yeah, yeah."

With purse in hand, she stepped out into the hallway. TJ followed. They waited in front of the elevators.

"Is there a reason I should be concerned about Franklin?"

She laughed, then looked at the agent. He was serious. "Sorry. No."

"He seemed a bit possessive."

"Drew is just angry."

"About what?"

The doors to the elevator opened up, and she waited until they stepped into it before answering.

"Drew is mad at all kinds of things, but mainly that life can suck sometimes."

"You care about him."

She nodded. "But as a friend...like a brother. He's been in

love with Cat for years, but that sort of went to crap. Now they are both dealing with the ramifications from a few months ago."

"Good."

She wanted to ask what that meant, but the doors opened and some more people got onto the lift. She had to step close and her hand brushed against his. He jerked at the contact, then looked down at her. He had felt the little jolt too. Good. Still, he said nothing, but he did take hold of her hand.

And that was enough for now.

The sun was just starting to sink over the water as Emma sat on their lanai and worked. She loved this little patch of happiness she and Del shared in Hawaii Kai, and couldn't wait to bring their baby home in a few weeks. At the thought, she felt her baby move and smiled as she rubbed her hand over her stomach. But the happiness didn't last long. Her smile faded, and she looked at her computer screen again. Something was really bothering her.

Emma nibbled on her bottom lip as she got back to work. She knew Charity wouldn't be happy with her snooping. Usually, Emma would honor her friend's wishes, but something in her gut told her that Callahan wasn't as innocent as he seemed. There was something in his expression, his gaze, that told her there were hidden depths to him. Sometimes that was a good thing. But, in this instance, she wasn't ready to let her friend take a chance.

"Hey," Del said as he sat down beside her at the patio table. "What are you working on?"

"Doing a little research,"

She was avoiding the truth on purpose. Del had strict rules about right and wrong. He saw hacking into a federal agency as against the law. Emma thought it depended on the reasons.

"On what?" he asked.

She glanced over at him. Before she had fallen in love with him, she would have had no problem lying to him. She was what her brother called a professional liar and she was good at it. Now though...she looked at her computer screen.

"Emma," he said, the soft warning in his voice was easy to hear.

"What?"

"Come on."

She sighed and turned to him again. There was no way out of it. He would always be able to tell when she was lying to him. These days, Del could sniff out the littlest of fibs.

"I don't like Callahan."

Del frowned. "You barely spoke to him."

She slanted him a look before looking out over the water.

"Okay. Tell me."

She might not be able to lie to him anymore, but Del always respected her gut reaction to people. It had served her well the years she had lived on the streets.

"There's something off. You've been complaining for months that we don't have a liaison, and they gave you the run around. Now, all of a sudden, some dude is just dropped into our laps."

"Maybe they just finally found the right one."

She shook her head. "Don't think that *gee shucks ma'am*

attitude is real. The things I'm reading about the wanker are what I would call...out of his field of expertise."

"What do you mean?"

She pulled up the info she had found on Callahan. "Here, he is part of something called Operation Money Wash. It was a covert kind of op."

"Why do you say that?"

"There is no official explanation in his files and I really can't find anything else out about the op."

"Wait, what? How did you get that?"

"I might have bruised a few laws."

He rolled his eyes. "Emma."

"Listen, they won't find me. You know I can hack better than anyone, other than Charity. Well, I am better, but not by much. But the problem is still there. He was part of an undercover op that's not mentioned in his official record. That makes me think he might be doing something now."

Del had opened his mouth to complain to her, but he snapped it shut. "You might be right."

"And that makes me wonder, why would they need to do that at all? Does the FBI think we are doing something illegal?"

"Other than hacking into their server?"

"Right. The fact that Charity is going out with him tonight bothers me too."

He studied her for a second, and Emma knew he was working through the information. "Okay, now you have *me* worried."

"It won't hurt to check it out and if it's nothing, we can just forget about it. But if he is dating my friend because of an investigation, then we need to know."

He was silent for a few minutes, then he nodded. "I will pretend I don't know you are doing it, but be careful."

"I will."

He leaned forward to kiss her forehead. "How about some pasta and red sauce tonight?"

She smiled. "That sounds smashing."

"Good. Do some work and I'll make dinner."

He left her alone as she started pounding on the computer keys. Emma hoped for all their sakes that she didn't find anything. But, if she did, she would make sure to make this Callahan cry. Investigating them was one thing, but using Charity like that would not be accepted.

TFH protected their own, and no dumbass FBI agent was going to be allowed to hurt Charity. Emma would make sure of it.

Chapter Five

Charity smiled as TJ pulled out into the Honolulu traffic. It was a stereotypical balmy night in Hawaii, and she had come to love them. She didn't mind her roots in the south, but it was nice that it wasn't ninety degrees out even after sundown. No matter what the day had been like or how hot it had gotten, the nights were beautiful the majority of the time.

"I didn't ask what kind of food you like."

She glanced over at TJ. He looked completely at ease in his dark blue shirt and khaki shorts—standard date clothes. One thing she liked about Hawaii is that it was so laid back. There was time for dressing up, and you could do it all you wanted. But there was no push for people to get gussied up, and she thanked God every day that people did not regularly wear pantyhose.

"I don't really care. Surprise me."

He gave her that grin, the one that showed his dimples and made his gray eyes twinkle.

"You got it."

He turned down a side street that led to Dillingham. When he pulled into the parking lot for a small local restaurant hidden from the bustling crowds of Ala Moana Avenue and Waikiki, she smiled. It was one of her favorite places to eat, since Drew had taken her the first week on the island. It wasn't fancy in the least. Older diner type of chairs with old tables littering the dining room area, and the menu rarely changed. It was clean and efficiently run, and if a person was looking for real local food, this was definitely one spot to hit.

After placing their order, she smiled.

"I wasn't sure how many *haoles* know this place exists."

He shrugged. "I made sure to find a few local places wherever I work."

"I'm the same way. When I lived in DC, I used to hit this little mom and pop place over in Centreville that served my favorite gyros."

"Anthony's on Centreville Road?" he asked.

"Yes."

He smiled. "Yeah, I loved that place. The owners have another place in Manassas that does a damned good breakfast."

"Oh, I didn't know that. I did like their Italian food, but I think Bravo's over near the Pearlridge Mall outdoes them."

"I haven't tried that yet."

"It's one of my favs. But that is a fair bit away from you. You live in Waimanalo you said?"

He hesitated and she wondered about it. "Yeah. I bought a rundown crack house."

"Second business?"

The bark of laughter surprised her. "No. I'm rehabbing it."

"A man of varied talents."

"Indeed."

"So, if you are doing that, I guess you aren't moving any time soon."

He shrugged. "I don't plan on it, much to my mother's irritation."

"Oh, I get that too. Mama isn't happy her baby girl is halfway across the world."

"I get that from Mom, even though she has three other sons to keep her busy. I want to set down roots, at least for a little while."

"Me too. I don't know what it was, but when I landed here, it all clicked. I've never been one for hot weather, but I love the way the sun here feels on my skin. And nothing beats the nights."

"Yes. Humidity is a bit much, but no worse than San Antonio, and definitely not as freaking hot."

"So, what made very special agent TJ Callahan come to Hawaii?"

He studied her for a second. "What makes you think I chose to come here?"

"Remember, I worked for the CIA." His eyebrows rose. "Of course I knew you knew I worked there. I would assume the FBI has a dossier on each of us. I also understand that this would be considered a prime assignment."

"That would depend on your reasons. A lot of people wouldn't like it because it doesn't help a lot of career fields."

"But you're in cyber."

"Right. And there is a lot here thanks to the hackers. Therefore, it won't hurt me working here."

"So why did you pick coming here?"

She had a feeling he didn't like her probing questions. With any other man, she might let it go, but for some reason, Charity didn't want to. Right now she wanted to know everything about him, and that wasn't her normal way of handling men. She saw each man she dated as a gift. Some were big bursts of fun, the type of present she delighted in for just a short time. Others, the joy stuck around longer. But, as she had when she was a little girl, she liked to unwrap her gifts slowly and extend the pleasure. For her, right now, she wanted to know every damned thing about him—and that was definitely odd.

He waited while their server delivered their drinks. "I wanted something different. I'd spent a lot of time in DC and Boston. LA was always a choice, but at this point in my life, I thought Hawaii would be fun."

She nodded. "Yeah, no kids, no spouse. Makes it easier to move over here."

"Exactly. And while I wouldn't mind sharing it with someone, it is pretty cool to be able to pick up and just go here or there on the islands. And your reason?"

"Control freak."

He blinked. Damn the man had the most amazing long eyelashes she had seen on a male. His eyes were light gray, and his dark brown lashes should look feminine and make him a bit too pretty. But, it was a direct contrast with the rugged appearance he presented the world—making him even more interesting to her.

"Excuse me?" he asked.

"From the time I was able to walk, my mama said I liked to control the entire house. And I did to a point. I'm a control freak. I hated working for the federal government because I always had what I called overlords."

"Overlords?"

"You know the type. The supervisors who like to watch every test you do, write you up for even the smallest infraction. At the CIA, there were so many of them. Not one of them gave a crap about me or my career, except how it affected their chances of moving up. Here, I have freedom to do what I want, plus, I'm teaching some courses at UH next fall. Lots of free time, and I have an apartment where I can see the ocean. Life is much better here."

He chuckled. "I have to agree with that. And your living arrangements?"

She had to roll her eyes. "Drew was shot a few months ago, but you know that."

"Yes. I was reading over the report, and Adam said he died at least once."

She sighed. "That kind of shook him up, and we were all understanding, but he has been pushing it lately. He's been moping around my apartment for too long. For living in Hawaii, I am pretty sure he hasn't been in the sun for more than a few minutes in the last month. I get him out of the house, but then he does his thing and heads back in. He always spent his weekends at the beach. He might end up at a beach, but only in a game."

"He doesn't have family on the island?"

"You mean you don't know?"

The blank look on his face was almost comical.

"Oh, give over. I know you have backgrounds on all of us. I just said that."

He shrugged, and she was growing to like the gesture.

"I have one, but since he's been out on medical leave, I hadn't read it over yet."

"Fair enough. And yes, he does have family. In fact, you're sitting in one of their restaurants."

He blinked and looked around. "He's part of the Chen family?"

The Chens were known for the restaurants not only on Oahu, but also on Maui and Kauai. "Yep. On his mother's side. In fact, his cousin is our server. Aren't you, Gail?"

The older woman smiled at her. "Yeah. And how is Drew doing?"

"A little better."

Which was a bit of a lie. Drew had been spiraling downward for months, but it wasn't something you shared while your waitress looked dead on her feet. The entire Chen family had been worried about Drew. It was understandable considering what he had been through, but their worry seemed to make Drew surlier.

When they were alone, TJ gave her an unblinking stare. She realized that she never wanted to sit on the other side of the interrogation table from Agent Callahan. He seemed laid back and easy going, but that look told her he was one serious man when it came to getting the truth.

"What?"

"You were lying."

"I was not."

He just smiled.

"Okay," she said leaning forward and whispering. "I was, but it's best they don't know."

"They are his family."

"So am I. And something needs to snap him out of his funk."

He nodded as he dug into his Lau Lau. They had both ordered the Hawaiian delicacy. Pork and butterfish were wrapped in a taro leaf, then steamed for six hours. She hadn't been so sure the first time she tried it, but she was a southern girl who grew up on chitlins, so she would try anything once.

"So, you like your work with TFH?"

She nodded. "Like I said, I prefer to be in charge."

"I thought Del was in charge."

"We just tell him that to make him feel better about himself. His ego needs help."

TJ chuckled. "Yeah, a former special ops Army guy, now the head of a unique group of investigators...he needs help with that."

"He was so sad when he first got here. Didn't know how to assert himself."

"Oh, I can imagine."

"So, you're from Texas?"

He nodded. "Dad was a Texas Ranger, as are three of my brothers."

"Three brothers?" Did they all look like him? Good lord.

"Yeah," he said slowly.

"What?"

"Nothing."

"No, there is something."

"Nothing much, just that...okay, it is a lot to live down being a Callahan. Lots of Rangers in our family. I used to have a knee jerk reaction when people would start asking me why I didn't become one."

She studied him for a long moment before responding. "I

get it. You wanted to do your own thing. Texas is a big state, but I can imagine that a lot of people in the Rangers know each other. Just like in the FBI."

"Yeah. I'm the oldest, and Dad was still active when I graduated from A&M. I really didn't want people to think I got the job because of my dad."

"Makes sense. I wouldn't like that either."

"What about your family?"

"I would think you would know."

He stilled and his face went blank again. "Why do you say that?"

"I told you, I knew that you would have files on us. I figured you knew about my family."

He seemed to let loose a breath, and his expression relaxed. "Yeah. You don't mind?"

She shook her head. "It's part of the job, and you can't work for the CIA and not expect it."

He nodded. "I didn't want to offend you."

"So, you know about my grandfather?"

"Uh, I am not sure what you are talking about."

"Grandpa Jackson insists he was in the Black Panthers."

"I didn't see anything in your file about that."

"I asked about it at the CIA too. They had no idea what I was talking about. I looked for years and couldn't find anything. He is going to be so disappointed when he finds out no one has a record of it."

"Really?"

"He boasts that he was listed on the FBI watch list, or whatever they called it back in the day."

"I have to say that I would have remembered that from your file."

She shook her head. Her grandfather would definitely be upset if he knew. "I just won't tell him."

"So, you're an only child."

She nodded. "Mom wasn't able to have any after me, and my father said I was enough to handle. I had a very weird upbringing."

"How?"

"I grew up in Atlanta society, which meant I was a deb, but with no boys in the family, my father taught me how to hunt and fish. I can pour a great cup of tea and I know how to dress a deer."

"I bet he doesn't regret that."

"Nope. He says I was the one thing that kept the family together."

"How is that?"

"My father is white. And not just white, but old Southern money white. Like in, his family probably owned slaves to work on their plantation. My mom is black, with a father who likes to run around telling people he was a Black Panther. My grandparents did not—do not—get along. Mom and Dad actually eloped because the stress of dealing with both families was too much. My grandfather refused to acknowledge my father, and my grandmother just could not forgive her son for not having a proper wedding."

"But you changed that?"

"Grandchildren always do, right? My grandmother had no daughters, then I come along. It just took one visit and my grandmother forgave them—as did my grandpa."

He smiled that full smile, the one the reached his eyes. "That sounds like you did save the family."

"Ah, they would have worked it out. Those two mellowed

as they got older. They still hate each other, but they pretend not to when we are together for holidays."

He just kept staring at her as if she had told the greatest story ever, so she asked, "Are you going to tell me what your real name is?"

His smile faded. "My name is TJ."

She couldn't fight the small smile. "Really?"

"You don't believe me?"

She shrugged. "Maybe, but now that was actually an odd reaction to a simple question."

"I get a lot of crap about it at work, too."

Not a complete lie, but there was something else there. It was beneath the surface, something he didn't reveal to just anyone. No worries on her part, because she could always find things out—and she would find out. She decided to change the subject.

"You said your father was in the Rangers. What does he do now?"

"They own a comic book shop in San Antonio. Well, a suburb outside of San Antonio."

"What?" She closed her eyes and sighed. When she opened them, TJ was looking at her as if she had lost her mind. "Be still my heart. Your parents are the owners of Ranger Comics?"

"Heard of them?"

"Of course I have. They're fantastic. I have never been, but I've special ordered from them. Wow."

"Small world," he murmured as he scooped up another forkful of his Lau Lau.

"The comic world is. And you said all three brothers are in the Texas Rangers?"

"Yeah."

"I just can't imagine what it was like raising four boys."

"There is a gap between us. I was around for several years before the other losers came along."

She smiled. "Relationships between brothers are always fascinating."

"How so?"

"Well, you all call each other names, put each other down. But there is no doubt in my mind that you would fight anyone who dared to threaten one of your brothers. And vice versa."

"Guilty, but I think that is the way of family."

She nodded. "Yep."

"In fact, that's the way of it for TFH. Or that's the feeling I get."

"Yes, I think of them as family. It's funny because I worked with the CIA for longer, and I didn't make one friend there. Not a close one. I wouldn't hesitate to call someone from TFH if I needed help."

"It was the CIA. How can anyone trust their coworkers there?"

She laughed. "I forgot about the interagency bitchiness of DC, but I think you are right. Hard to trust spies, even if you were one yourself."

"Especially if you are one."

She sighed. "Yeah. But, here, it's different."

"That makes you lucky."

"I know that, and I relish it. Truth is, I would lay down my life for any of them and I know they would do the same for me."

"That says a lot about TFH."

"Yeah it does. But then, you probably read into that when you snooped on us."

For a second he didn't say anything, but in the next instant, he threw back his head and laughed. Feeling even more relaxed, she sipped her water and smiled. She didn't know where this was going, or even if it was going anywhere, but Charity was sure she would enjoy the ride.

TJ accompanied her on the elevator up to her apartment. She had told him he didn't need to, but his mother had raised him right. Plus, he wanted a few more minutes in her company. It was probably a bad idea to get this infatuated with her. Even if he wasn't on the job, he didn't often fall this fast for a woman. A smart man would walk away and just be friendly. For the first time in his career, he was having a problem doing just that.

"I had a really good time tonight," she said, as she stepped off the elevator and into the hallway.

"I did too."

And then he said nothing else. He couldn't. His mind had gone blank, as it had a few times during the date. For some reason, his palms were sweating and his heart was thumping hard against his chest. Hell, there was a good chance he might pass out if he wasn't careful about it. He was more nervous than he had been the first time he had approached a girl to ask her out.

"I would like to do it again, if you're open to it."

He should say no. First, he rarely had women pursue him. It was probably old fashioned, but he liked to be the one who initiated interaction. Secondly, during the date, he had realized he wanted more than just the investigation. If she turned up clean, he wanted a real date. But, as he had proven throughout the day, he didn't always think straight when it came to Charity.

"I'd like that too."

She stopped at her door and smiled up at him. "Thanks again for tonight."

She leaned in close, and he could catch her scent then. Lavender. With the smoothest of moves, she brushed her mouth against his and was pulling away before he was ready. Just a simple taste, one that called to something in him. Something primal. Instinct took over. He slipped his hands around her waist and drew her closer, deepening the kiss.

He slanted his mouth over hers again and again. The small moan she released sunk into his blood and caused the ancient beat of lust to grow louder. The world faded away. He wanted her. Right there. Right then. Without thinking, he pressed himself closer. His cock strained against the zipper of his cargo pants.

Charity wrapped her leg around his and slid it against his. Now. It had to be now. Then, he heard a door shut down the hall. Reality crashed down onto the pleasant lust-fueled moment, and he forced himself to step back.

She frowned, and without opening her eyes, she moved closer to him, but he stopped her.

"Charity."

Her eyes fluttered open, then he saw the heat in her cheeks.

"Well...that definitely escalated quickly."

He smiled. "Yeah, it did." He couldn't resist her swollen

lips, so TJ swooped down for one more quick kiss. "I'll call you tomorrow."

She nodded. "Thanks for dinner."

"You are more than welcomed. Good night."

She didn't move. "You could come in for a drink."

Yes. Yes. *Yes.*

But he shook his head. "No. I think we both know it won't be just a drink, and I am not sure either of us is ready for that step yet."

"Okay. But..."

"No," he said with a laugh. "Now, go on, so I know you're inside."

She nodded and unlocked the door. "Night, TJ."

"Night, Charity."

Once he heard her shut the door, he waited for the lock. He knew she had Drew in there with her, but he still wanted to make sure. Once he heard it, he started back to the elevator. Now that he had gotten to know Charity, he wasn't sure she was the person they wanted. Yes, part of it was his own personal feelings for her. She was funny, gorgeous, smart, and damn, he loved that laugh of hers.

There was also a streak of pride. Not arrogance, but pride in her work. It was odd all the way around that she would be tied up in something with Foley. A woman like her was a little too smart—common sense wise—to fall for Foley.

With a sigh, he stepped onto the elevator. He needed to find out the questions to the answers and do it soon. He needed to make sure of who she was before they made it into bed. Truth was, he would have broken his rule about first dates with women like Charity. If there hadn't been an investigation going on, he might have just let her persuade him into bed.

But he had a job, and he couldn't risk screwing it up.

Charity practically danced into work the next morning. She was still buzzing from the date with TJ. It was so amazing to have met a man who thought like she did. When she stepped into the room, she found Adam, Del and Emma. She did not like the look all of them were giving her.

"What's up?"

"I think you need to sit down," Adam said. He was using that voice he used to keep people calm. That was so not a good sign.

"Tell me what's going on."

"I'll tell you what is going on," Emma growled. "That Hammer person is a bastard."

Charity blinked. "What?"

Emma opened her mouth, but Del stepped in. "Listen, apparently Hammer is officially our liaison with the FBI, but Emma did some digging and found out things about him."

"What kind of things?"

"He's looking into all of us, but especially you."

"And how is that different than when you met Del? Lord knows, you probably hacked Del's file before you came to work here."

"Emma didn't do that."

Emma stayed quiet. Then, he looked at her.

"Dammit, Emma."

"I didn't do it. I told you about this. Sean did it."

Emma's brother was a security expert and was overly protective of his sister.

Del shook his head. "Your situation is different. Emma found digital fingerprints on your leave records, your financial records, and your personal computer."

Charity's mind went blank. She just could not think straight.

"Also," Emma said, "I talked to a few of my friends. You remember the name Foley?"

"Yeah. He's wanted by the FBI and Europol. He finds himself an idiot to use…"

The moment it sank in, Charity stomach turned.

"Oh no."

"Oh, yes," Emma said.

"He thinks I'm the idiot."

Emma stepped closer and rubbed her hand down Charity's arm. For a woman who had issues with physical contact, it meant a lot that she was trying to sooth Charity. It also told her that the situation was completely screwed up.

"But we know that isn't true."

She looked at Del. "I'm sorry."

"This isn't your fault. We're going to have to work out what is going on here, and why they latched onto you. For right now, I want you to pretend everything is the same."

"I'm horrible at that. Maybe I'll just avoid him."

"That will make him suspicious. He will think you're avoiding him because of guilt."

She wanted to growl. "Dammit. This isn't fair."

"Give Emma a little more time, and I'm going to talk to a few people I know. We will get this cleared up."

"Then Del can beat him up."

"Emma," Del said, "please stop telling people I can beat other people up."

"What? I would do it but I'm pregnant."

Charity shook her head. "I don't want to beat him up."

"Oh, come on. Maybe you want to hurt him a little bit?"

She sighed. "No, not physically. But I do want to make him look like an idiot."

"Good, because I plan on doing that. I'll talk to some friends, Del is going to talk to some of his contacts, and Marcus is going to talk to Tamilya. She still has some contacts at the FBI. By the time this is done, we will make him feel as if he is the stupidest man at the FBI, and that is saying a lot."

"Thanks. I-I need a few moments."

"Sure," Del said. "And feel free to take some personal time today."

She nodded and walked out of the office, her mind still spinning from the revelations. It wasn't like she was in love with TJ, but the one thing she valued was the truth. He had lied to her...and worse...he had used her. He could have turned her down, and he didn't need to kiss her the way he had the night before.

And for that, she would gladly make him cry. But first, she thought as she stepped off the elevator, she was going to give herself permission to wallow. Because, while she might not have been in love with him, it didn't mean being used hurt any less.

Chapter Six

TJ spent the next morning going through the piles of information about Charity. There was something that had been bugging him since he had gotten the first financial reports. Charity seemingly had a lot of money. It was usually a red flag. She didn't have a huge salary to explain the cash. Foley was very generous when he latched onto someone. Money or gifts were big and unexpected for the person he had targeted. So, it made sense that when a woman who earns a modest income buys an apartment worth close to a million dollars, the FBI took notice. Some superficial digging had uncovered a trust set up by her grandfather on her father's side. That explained the money she had to pay for that fantastic apartment.

Still, the connection the FBI made was bothering him. Why would their tracking show that she had a connection to Foley? There was only one breach. Granted, it was for operatives in the Far East, and the hack had been successful. It made him think that it wasn't the only hack—or there was more to come. Granted, they had assumed Foley sold the information after he acquired it, but from the report he read, there was no indication that had happened. After looking over her record, TJ had no doubt Charity could hack into the FBI computers. There was a problem with that. The woman was just too damned smart to get caught, let alone do it from her computer at work.

Irritated, he pushed away from his desk and stood. Rubbing the ache on the back of his neck, he looked out the window, not really seeing what was there. He knew there was some kind of connection he just wasn't making—and the FBI wasn't either. Truth was, he was wondering why Remington had latched onto her. It was out of character for him to jump to conclusions, but then, Remington hadn't been the same since their last run in with Foley.

A knock at the door broke into his turbulent thoughts.

"Come in," he said.

The door opened enough for his boss to pop his head in. "Hey, I just sent you the documentation on that Edwards woman. Looks like there is a good chance that she had nothing to do with the hack. I wanted to make sure you got it before I headed out to the airport."

"You going to DC?"

He winced. His boss hated meetings more than TJ did, and he particularly hated DC. He'd been born and raised in California, and after his stint at the Academy, Tsu had avoided DC as much as possible. "No, thank God. Seattle. Tech con they are making me attend."

TJ chuckled. "Have fun."

Another wince. "It's supposed to rain all week. And the

high is only going to be in the fifties. Who wants to live in weather like that?"

"Apparently a lot of people since Seattle is crowded."

"Mass insanity if you ask me. What's the use of living by the ocean if you can't surf?"

Tsu left TJ alone and he pulled up the docs. When he read through them, he knew that there was no way that she was the one helping Foley. He grabbed his phone and called Remington.

"I think we have an issue with Charity Edwards."

"How so?"

"I'm emailing you the information that Tsu gave me. Edwards was in LA at the time of the first hack. There is no way it was her."

He heard Remington clicking on his keyboard over the phone. "Hmm, yes, but we need this verified. There is no proof that she was there. I don't think we can dismiss her."

There was a tone in Remington's voice that TJ recognized. It was the obsession that had lead them down a dangerous path. TJ had gone along the last time, but he wasn't going to do it blindly. Mentors could also make mistakes, and Remington had been making his fair share of them the last few years. Last time, TJ had almost died because of it.

"No, but I would say you might want to find out who else would have access to the computers at TFH. Or, who could make it look like it was the computers at TFH. For some reason, someone wants us to think they are in league with Foley."

"That is if the Edwards woman is innocent. Right at the moment, I have my doubts."

He didn't like Remington's tone. As wonderful of a mentor as he was, he had his faults, and one of them was having tunnel vision. It helped him work a case to completion. But there were times where it could go badly for everyone involved.

"We could ask her. Just straight out. She strikes me as the kind of woman who would tell it like it is."

There was a long pause. "No. You know the drill. If you tell the woman, she might tell Foley and then he could disappear."

TJ leaned back in his chair and thought. Yes, his personal feelings were involved. It was hard to separate that. He couldn't remember the last time he'd been this attracted to a woman. He had never been a man for forbidden fruit, so he knew it wasn't that aspect that appealed to him. Charity just wasn't the type, not really. Every one of his marks had been needy. That was not a word he would apply to Charity Edwards.

Even though he had major doubts, he knew if he insisted on her innocence that Remington would pick up on it.

"Sure. I'll keep up my surveillance."

"You do that. I'm going to have some folks run down the information on her trip. I'm sure the airports have security footage. If she was there, she should show up."

"Sounds good."

Remington hung up once again without saying goodbye. TJ had grown accustomed to Remington's personality while he had been working for him. In the year he had been away from DC, TJ apparently had gotten out of practice. In the Hawaii Field Office, they did their jobs, but things were not as insane as in DC. It was one of the reasons he'd requested the position. After the craziness of the Foley investigation, he had needed a break.

Thinking of Foley brought him back to Charity. The sooner he cleared Charity, the sooner he could get serious about dating her. He felt guilty enough as it was going out last night with her. Another symptom of being away from DC. He didn't think twice about things like being untruthful with one of the most fascinating women he had ever met. So, maybe he could see if she was interested in a lunch date. He shook his head. Too soon. Maybe see if she wanted to go out on Friday night? That would be best.

He picked up the phone to call her, but someone else knocked on the door. Santos looked in. "We got a meeting in five."

"Tsu's not here."

"This is for that task force they are setting up for online predators."

Damn. "Okay. Forgot about that."

Yeah, because he was preoccupied with Charity. He gathered up his stuff he needed for the meeting. He'd call her after lunch.

Charity got through the morning with coffee and malasadas thanks to Adam. He had shown up without explanation with a box and a large cup of her favorite Kona.

"So, I take it you were called away because of Jin."

He nodded. "She's not getting better."

"What was it this time?"

"She'd been out drinking. Passed out in her car."

About a year ago, Jin had been abducted by a pair of sadistic bastards who had been raping, torturing, and killing women. She had been their only survivor. Charity would never dream of passing judgment on the way Jin had handled it. Truth was, Charity wasn't sure she could ever fathom the nightmare existence Jin had experienced for a week. To live with the memories, and know that everyone you're acquainted with knows, would be unbearable. Charity just wished there was something she could do to help Adam.

"Damn. Do you know if Elle has talked to her?"

"She's going to stop by today to check on her."

She nodded, and the door to her lab opened up. Marcus strode in, a look of irritation marring his usually pretty face. A slim, attractive black woman followed him. She was tall, at least four inches taller than Charity, and wore her hair slicked back in a French twist at the base of her neck. A heavy fringe of bangs covered her forehead. Dark brown eyes took in every aspect of the lab. Charity was pretty sure she was committing it to memory.

"I heard what happened," Marcus said.

Charity glanced past him to the woman.

"I'm Tamilya, since Marcus decided to ignore me."

"Woman, I'm not ignoring you."

Charity fought a smile. In all the time she had known Marcus, she had never seen him act this way toward anyone. "Nice to meet you. And this comment has nothing to do with you, but," she said directing her attention to Marcus, "I don't think we should talk about this in front of outsiders."

"I can wait in the hall, but Marcus wanted me to tell you about the Hammer."

"You know him from your time with the FBI?"

She nodded. "We went to Quantico at the same time."

Charity smiled. "Adam, give this woman a malasada."

"Oh, no," she said glancing at the box. Her eyes stayed on the box for a second longer than a regular glance, then she looked back at Charity. "I really shouldn't. But thanks."

"So, the Hammer?" she asked.

Tamilya nodded. "Yeah, well, he's kind of intense. Always has been."

"I get that."

"It was hard to be friendly at first. I'd been valedictorian at my high school and then third in my graduating class at the University of Alabama." Then she glanced around the office. "Ugh, you're a bulldog."

Charity laughed. "I didn't graduate. I got picked up by the CIA my sophomore year."

"Still," she said with an exaggerated sniff, then she smiled. "We are both very competitive, but he's a pretty good guy. One of those salt of the Earth types as my Mom says."

"That sounds about right."

"And, after the big mess a year ago, he has gotten even worse they say."

"Mess?"

"You mean you didn't hack..."

"I did no such thing." She hadn't. Emma had, but there was no reason to let her know that.

"Well, he was involved in some kind of undercover operation. I had just left the FBI, but I heard about it. He was on the task force to bring down Foley."

The pieces were all starting to fall into place. "I remember something about that operation. A woman was killed."

"Yes, and Hammer ended up in the hospital. He took it hard because Foley got away and a civilian was killed. Being a perfectionist can be hard when you work in law enforcement. Sometimes you win and sometimes you lose—and sometimes people die."

There was no need for Charity to ask, but Tamilya had experienced something similar to TJ. She knew she had left the FBI for a reason, but now she was getting an idea that it might have been a case gone wrong.

Charity sighed. "And now, all of a sudden, Foley has popped up here. This is all very weird."

"Yes."

"Do you think he was involved with Foley?" Marcus asked.

Tamilya snorted. "No."

"Why?" Adam asked.

"He's Captain Freaking America. Seriously. You know his family background?" Charity nodded. "They are the quintessential crime fighting family. He believes deeply in doing the right thing and telling the truth. That's why I was so surprised that he was put undercover. He is a kickass agent, but I never saw him being good at deception."

"Apparently he learned."

Just as she said it, her phone rang. Damn. Even now, her palms went sweaty and her pulse scrambled. It had to be anger...right? She couldn't still be attracted to a man who had deceived her.

"It's him."

"Are you going to answer?" Adam asked.

She drew in a breath and released it before picking up her phone. "Hey, there."

"How is your day going?"

"Not too bad," she said, adding a little sugar to her voice. Marcus' eyebrows shot up at it, but Charity ignored him.

"I was wondering if you wanted to go out again."

She didn't say anything at first. She let the invitation hang in the air.

"Sure. That sounds good."

"Are you free Friday night?"

"I am. In fact, Drew is supposed to have a night out with the boys."

"Sounds great. Seven good?"

"Seven is excellent."

"See you then."

She clicked off the phone.

"What the hell are you up to, Charity?" Adam asked.

"Del said to make him think I don't know. If I avoid contact with him, he might think I'm guilty. Besides, by Friday, I will have enough information."

Adam shook his head. "Men always think women are the weaker sex."

Tamilya crossed her arms. "And we have to prove you wrong every generation. You want to be careful with him, Charity."

"With Adam?"

"No. With Callahan. He is even-tempered and a hard worker, but I will tell you, the reason he is good at cyber is because he is good at zeroing in on the subject and not letting go. He can detect any little mistake, any hint of deception. Those types always have a trigger of some sort, and you might just flip it."

"I bet. But he never met the likes of me."

"You're not trained for undercover work," Marcus said.

Charity smiled. "Yeah, but I was raised by a smart woman. I know just how to give a man enough rope to hang himself. And this one is going to be worth every moment I get to watch him dangle."

Chapter Seven

The week seemed to fly by for Charity. She had so much going on with preparing for the trial that she should have had very little time to think about TJ. She wished it had worked that way. Each time she had a moment to catch her breath, TJ popped up in her head. Even when she should be paying attention to something, she found her thoughts straying to the agent. She dreaded the date.

"So, I hear we have a fed we need to beat up?" Cat said over the phone. She'd been gone visiting some family on Maui all week and had just gotten back.

"Not yet."

"Damn. I was aiming to let loose some demons."

"Bad trip?"

She sighed. "One half of the family wants me to be something other than a cop, and the other half is asking why I don't have a husband."

"You're only twenty-six."

"Yeah, well, when I had that date with Drew, they had high hopes for me. My usual dates are not to their liking."

"Ah."

Charity could see that. Drew came from a very influential family on the island. Not only did they have several restaurants in Hawaii, they had recently expanded to California and Japan. Beyond that, he had one or two family members in state politics. Most locals would see him as an eligible bachelor. Drew would rather everyone just leave him alone. The date had been to Del and Emma's wedding, and had ended with Drew being shot the next day. Since that point, Cat had avoided Drew and, at first, Charity had been pissed. But as time passed, she had realized something else was going on. She just wasn't sure what yet, but she was sure she would figure it out soon.

"I have a date tonight, and Drew is going out with the guys."

There was a beat of silence. "How's he doing?"

There. Right there. Charity heard it in Cat's voice. She knew what happened shook the whole team, but Cat had been shattered. She cared about Drew, though. "Better. I think in time we'll get the old Drew back."

Cat said nothing about that. "Tell you what. I'm in the office catching up on paperwork. I'll hang out here until you text me and let me know everything is done for the night."

"I really don't think you need to do that."

"I know you can handle yourself, but there is nothing wrong with a little backup."

"Thanks. I'll let you know."

"Talk later."

Charity hung up just as Drew stepped into her doorway.

"Hey, what time is the bastard picking you up?"

He was dressed for his night out in his favorite Doctor Who shirt and shorts. He had even combed his hair—which was never a sure thing these days.

"He'll be here in an hour and you will be gone."

He frowned at her. "You planned it that way."

Not a question. The boy was smart.

"Yes. You are not always that good at deception, and I know you're thinking about punching him."

"I *am* going to punch him."

She shook her head and turned to face him. "I need to pretend just a little bit longer. As soon as we get some more info on him and exactly why they are looking at me, we will hit him."

She studied him and realized that for the first time in months, Drew was more animated. It was the first thing she had associated with him. Full of life and not afraid so show his adorable dorky side.

"You look good."

"Thank you, my Ebony Queen."

She smiled at the use of his first nickname for her. He was showing her more and more of the old Drew. In the last few days, he seemed to be loosening up and wanting to get out of the apartment. She knew after the experience that he might not be exactly the same, but she wanted him to be happier.

"I'm not sure what I'm going to get out of tonight."

"Being out with friends. That's all you need. And, let's face it. Hanging out with me and my cats is not doing anything for your image. You need some male bonding time."

He smiled and this one reached his eyes. "Yeah."

The doorbell rang. "And on cue, that must be whoever is picking you up."

"Marcus."

"Oh, speaking of which," she said when she followed him out into the living area. "I met the very attractive Tamilya the other day."

He slanted her a look. "Yeah?"

She nodded. "She gave us some background on our FBI agent."

"Vibes?"

She knew what he was asking. Since they had seen the way Marcus Floyd reacted whenever there was a chance he would see the woman, they had known he had a thing for her. "There's an office pool, and the pot increased after her visit."

"I'm going to have to get in on that," he said.

He opened the door. Marcus was dressed for the night. A designer Hawaiian shirt and khaki shorts. It still amazed her she was surrounded by so many beautiful men, but had never been interested in any of them outside of friendship. She had chalked it up to the fact they were in law enforcement. Cops had never been her thing. At least, until the very deceptive Agent Callahan had popped up into her life, the bastard.

"Well, don't you look handsome. With you and Drew, you'll have to fight off the women."

Marcus rolled his eyes. "Guys night."

"Please tell me you aren't going out to a strip joint."

Marcus chuckled. "No, just dinner and some drinking. Do you need backup tonight?"

"I'm fine." She thought back to her conversation with Cat, but decided not to mention the conversation in front of

Drew. "I've got backup if I need it, but I don't think I'll have a problem."

"Good."

"Be careful with him, Charity," Drew said.

"I will. Don't worry."

Once she ushered them out of the apartment, she decided to get ready. TJ had texted her earlier today and asked if she would be up for a ride in his Jeep. She had agreed and tried to fight the niggle of admiration. A lot of men would just expect you to go along with them. Not TJ. It was actually very considerate of him.

With a sigh, she pushed the thought aside. He was the enemy, and he needed to be destroyed. But first, she would make sure she backed him to the edge of the cliff.

TJ stepped into the the elevator and pressed the button for Charity's floor. Tonight had taken on a different meaning after this week. He had researched her, the team, Foley, looked into all of their accounts, and he had yet to pick up on anything. Because of that, he had come a decision.

She was innocent.

He couldn't prove it completely, but right at the moment, he had no idea why the FBI had been led to her. He was sure now that it had been a set up of some sort, some way to throw them off the path of the real culprit. That had bothered him more than anything. Knowing that someone was using the FBI that way should be a concern to all of them, but TJ hadn't said a word to Remington. Without proof, there would be no way of swaying his old boss.

He walked down her hall, bracing for another interaction with her roommate. Drew wasn't a rival for her affections. He understood that. He wasn't stupid, and not once did he get a vibe of attraction between Drew and Charity. Still, the man was living with Charity, and that was enough to put TJ off. He got the definite feeling that Drew did not like him, and TJ knew that his opinion would matter a lot to Charity.

He raised his hand to knock on the door. It took her a few seconds to make it to the door. When it opened, he felt the air leave his lungs. The woman just took his breath away. Tonight she was wearing a red sleeveless blouse that she tied at her waist and a pair of jean shorts. He let his gaze travel down to her feet. Of course, her toe nails were painted. Red—a perfect match to her shirt.

"Is there something wrong?"

He tore his gaze away from her feet. She was smiling.

"Sorry. No, nothing wrong."

Other than the fact that he was overly turned on by the fact that she had painted her toe nails. It was a bit embarrassing, especially since he had never been a foot man.

Charity said nothing. She slipped on a pair of black sandals—or slippahs as the locals called them.

"Where are Jess and Luke?"

She rolled her eyes. "They're mad. Drew is out with the guys and left them on their own. They are protesting by sleeping on his bed." She grabbed her purse and stepped out into the hallway, locking the door.

"Ready?"

More than she would ever know. He wanted this damned investigation over with because he really wanted to see where

Constant Craving

they were headed. He pushed those thoughts aside and nodded.

"It's a gorgeous night."

She laughed and pulled out a scarf from her purse.

"There is one thing you can be certain of. Unless we have a tropical storm or hurricane hitting, most nights are beautiful in Hawaii."

Drew looked down the table and smiled. Charity had been correct. Getting out with the guys was just the right thing. They'd picked a bar and grill in Waikiki known for their fish tacos.

"So, what is your take on the FBI dude?" Marcus asked.

"Not sure. I thought he really had a thing for her."

"He could. Doesn't mean he isn't investigating her," Marcus said.

"You know him?"

Marcus nodded. "Yeah. Not well, that's for sure. Not sure anyone really knew him well. I didn't know his family had a rep in the Texas Rangers."

"What do you mean?" Del asked.

"He's had a family member in the Texas Rangers since it's inception."

"Wow."

"Yeah. Generations there. But he never said a word about it. Most guys I know would have been telling anyone who would listen. Not a peep. I only know because Tamilya knew about it."

"Charity said they went to Quantico together," Del remarked.

"Yeah. And he was the top of the class, but he kept to himself. Very quiet. No one was surprised when he was tapped to work with cyber."

"That is definitely curious," Drew said.

Del narrowed his eyes. "How much have you had to drink?"

"Just two beers. This is my third."

"You might want to be careful. Have you had a drink since you've been out of the hospital?"

He shook his head and the scenery revolved around him. "Yeah, I better lay off it."

"Anyway, I think Emma has all the info we need, but her brother said he had something for her. I think we might be ready to pin him to the wall."

"You're pretty mad about this," Marcus commented.

"You're damned right I am. Bastard came into our house. *Our house.*" He slammed his hand down on the table causing some of the glasses to jump. It wasn't that often Del lost his temper like that. "And, going after one of our Ohana? That is unforgivable."

As if on cue, Del's phone went off. "Emma."

He was quiet as he listened to his wife. His frown deepened, and his expression grew more stark.

"Are you sure?"

More silence. When Emma was excited, she often spoke so fast it was hard to understand her, but somehow, the boss always seemed to comprehend.

"Okay, I'll talk it over with the team. Get some rest."

"And what did she say?" Adam asked after Del hung up.

Constant Craving

"You mean other than telling me to get bent when I told her to rest?"

Marcus chuckled. "That woman has not changed one bit since getting pregnant."

"And she has the information we need. We'll play it close to our chest, but we will make sure to let him hoist himself on his own petard."

They had taken a drive to the other side of the island and watched the sun sink below the horizon as they did. She had tried the entire time to pretend it was for real. It would have been a perfect date in her mind. Laidback was her style. Oh, she liked a little romance, and sometimes big gestures, but she had been raised in the South. She appreciated the quiet times with people she enjoyed.

"You've been awfully quiet," TJ remarked as they started eating their meals. He'd taken her to a small fish taco place—another local favorite. If he wasn't a deceptive butthead, she would be totally into him. Okay, she *was* into him, but she did have standards. Standards that at the moment seemed to be wavering. She knew he was on the job, but he was so damned sweet.

"I just had a rough week. I get preoccupied when I have a court case coming up."

"I hate court too."

"Yeah?"

He nodded as he chewed and swallowed a bite of his taco. "I don't like being put on display. I know a few guys who have gotten out of the FBI and been hired on as expert witnesses. They always loved sitting up there testifying. Not my thing."

"Mine either. Some of the technical and scientific stuff is just above everyone's head. The blank stares from the jury always make me freak out. The first case I testified in, I had a panic attack. It was a disaster."

He smiled. Just a simple curving of the lips. Even knowing what she did, understanding that he couldn't be trusted, it got to her. He got to her. He was practically made for her. Looks and personality perfect for her. That is until she thought about how he was investigating her.

"So, Drew is out with the men of TFH tonight?"

She nodded. "I was worried he would avoid it, but he seemed gung ho tonight."

"That's good."

They ate in silence for a minute to two. Usually, she would freak out. Charity always liked noise, chatter. Mostly, she loved to talk, but she didn't like long silences. With TJ, it was different. And that worried her. The fact that she was so damned comfortable with him should make her happy, but of course, with their situation, it did not.

"I thought we could head back down Pali. I always liked that road at night."

She smiled. "Sounds like a great plan."

This was going to kill her. She couldn't be herself, but she couldn't really be comfortable around him. She had been a deb, so she knew exactly how to be in fact. Smiles, kisses on the cheek—she had learned to master the art of socializing at the elite Southern gatherings. And, if she didn't have feelings for him, she would be so pissed that she would be able to pull it off.

"Are you sure nothing's wrong?"

She looked up at him. God. Concern darkened those gorgeous gray eyes.

She shook her head. "Like I said, it was a long week, and I am not looking forward to next week."

"Well, then," he leaned over and brushed his mouth against hers.

It wasn't a full kiss. In most cases, she wouldn't even call it a kiss. With TJ, she felt it all the way to her soul. It rocked her foundation. When he pulled back, a strange mixture of arousal and shame washed over her. He was lying to her, using her, and she was attracted to him.

"I hoped that would make you feel better."

She opened her eyes and looked at him. He definitely looked upset, and a small part of her, the stupid part of her who was still attracted to the geek with the hot body, took over.

"No. I'm just trying to figure out how I'm attracted to a man who would pick Captain America over Iron Man."

His expression lightened and he shook his head. "Iron Man. Really?"

She chuckled. "Captain America is such a goody two shoes."

"Tony Stark is an asshole."

"A very attractive asshole," she said.

With a sigh, he grabbed his drink. "At least we agree that Matt Smith has been the best Doctor."

She stared at him without saying a word.

"Don't tell me you're a Tennant fan."

"Okay, I won't."

"What could you possibly see in him?"

Pushing aside the real reason she was there, she started to debate TJ about the finer qualities of the tenth Doctor. Reality would arrive soon enough.

They stepped off the elevator and walked down the hall to her door again. It had been a pleasant night, but TJ knew something was wrong. Really wrong. She had engaged with him, but he felt as if she were holding back. In fact, until they started arguing about superheroes and Doctor Who, she had seemed almost detached.

"I had a great time again," Charity said, giving him a smile. It didn't reach her eyes. Alarm bells were going off in his head. There was something definitely wrong.

"Is there something wrong?"

Her eyes widened. "No. Sorry. I'm really worried about that case on Monday. The lawyer for the defendant and I have a history."

"Oh."

"But I had a really great time tonight. Truly."

Something loosened in his chest, and he found himself able to take another deep breath.

He stepped closer, bent his head close just as her door flung open. He glanced over before a fist shot out and hit him square in the jaw. He hadn't been ready for it so he stumbled back.

"*Drew*," Charity yelled.

"Fuck," was all he could say when he fell back against the wall. His head slammed into the light fixture and bright flashes of stars appeared before his eyes. Pain radiated from his jaw.

"What are you doing?" Charity yelled.

"Defending your honor," Drew said stepping closer. She positioned herself between the two of them, as if he needed someone to defend him.

"First of all, I don't need any defending. I can take care of my own honor."

A door down the hallway opened, and Charity muttered something under her breath.

"Both of you inside now."

He opened his mouth to refute her, but she pushed Drew as she grabbed TJ by the shoulder. She dragged him into her apartment and kicked the door shut.

"Do you want to explain to me what that was about, Drew?" she demanded.

"Not really," Drew said.

"Well, I'm going to have to insist on it," TJ said, and instantly regretted it. His fucking jaw hurt.

"I don't think you have a leg to stand on as they say, Callahan. Fucking with Charity? You think you won't end up paying for that?"

His words were slightly slurred. TJ got a whiff of beer and realized Drew had probably had a bit too much to drink. Then, what Drew said hit TJ.

Everything in him stilled. He glanced at Charity, who wasn't looking at him. The sound of rushing water seemed to fill his ears, as he looked from Charity to Drew—who still stood with his hands fisted ready to strike again—then back to Charity.

"Charity?"

She sighed and looked at him. The moment stretched out, and he knew the expression in her eyes. It was pity and resignation. The bottom of his stomach seemed to dissolve in that one instant.

"We know you're investigating me."

"Well, shit."

Chapter Eight

After a call to the boss that had not gone well, Charity returned to the living room. She looked at both men. TJ was holding his jaw and ignoring Drew. Jess comforted him while Drew sat on the couch with Luke by his side. The cats in her life were evenly split.

How had her life turned crazy in less than two weeks? She had been happy working in her little lab, playing with evidence. Now, she had two angry men in her apartment, an FBI investigation focusing on her, and her boss was coming over to tear someone a new asshole. There was only one thing she knew at the moment. It was *not* going to be her butt on the line.

TJ moved his jaw from side to side. She sighed. She might be pissed at both of them but her mother had raised her right. After getting herself a drink of water, Charity grabbed a frozen bag of peas and handed them to TJ.

"Del is on his way over." She glanced at Drew. "He's not happy with you."

"Yeah, well..." he sighed.

The attack was so out of character for Drew, so she knew something else was going on. He wasn't a man prone to violence. As the geek, she was sure he talked his way out of things rather than fought, and he definitely didn't start fights.

"Did you drink tonight?" He nodded. "How much?"

"Four beers."

She threw up her hands in disgust. "Drew, that's way too many. You haven't drunk since you got out of the hospital, and you were never a heavyweight."

"Still doesn't change the fact that the bastard was investigating you."

She glanced at TJ, who had said almost nothing since she'd told him they knew about the investigation. Then she looked at Drew. "He could have you arrested for assaulting him. He's a federal agent."

Drew's expression turned mulish. He glanced around her. "But he won't, will you, Callahan? Because our agent friend knows that he would have to explain the situation, or I would. And it would look bad for the FBI."

She stepped into his line of vision. She waited until Drew's attention was on her again. "Either way. Del said that we were going to deal with this Monday."

"How long have you known?" TJ asked.

The anger vibrating in his voice fed her own. The man had a lot of nerve to be pissed at her. She turned to face him.

"Since Tuesday."

"But you still went out with me." Disgust dripped from every word.

"Oh, don't judge me if you aren't ready to cast a shadow

on yourself, *Agent* Callahan. I didn't know the first time we went out. You asked me out and played me from the beginning."

"I did not ask you first. *You* asked me."

She opened her mouth to refute the comment, but the truth was there. Sure, he had asked her for coffee, but she was the one who suggested dinner.

"Still."

He snorted, then winced.

"Serves you right," she said as her doorbell rang. She stalked over to the door. Del stood there alone.

"Oh good. I was afraid you wouldn't be able to get away without Emma."

"Her brother is with her, and he convinced her to stay home. It wasn't that easy, and she wants to kick some FBI ass, as she put it." She stepped back to let him in. He walked in, looked at TJ, then Drew. "Tell me what happened."

Drew opened his mouth, but she shook her head. "I went out with Callahan, but you knew that was happening tonight. I was thanking him for the nice evening."

Drew snorted this time.

"And this buffoon opened the door and sucker-punched Callahan."

Del shook his head. "Couldn't wait until Monday?"

Drew shrugged. "I was pissed."

"You had too much to drink tonight. I told you to stop on that third beer." He looked at TJ. "Of course, now you know. Is there anything we need to act on tonight? Can this wait until Monday?"

He nodded.

"Do you need a ride home?"

The look TJ gave him would have withered a lesser man, but Del was made of tough stock.

"I got it."

"Monday morning, my office, eight a.m."

TJ nodded. He handed her the peas.

"Thanks."

She nodded. He said nothing else as he walked out the door. Once they were alone, the silence almost deafened her.

She cleared her throat. "What did Emma find out tonight?"

"They went full throttle on you. Expenses, they even made inquiries into how you paid for this apartment. They looked into everything, including every man you've seen in the last few months."

She swallowed. "Damn."

"Don't worry. They couldn't find anything. All they had from the beginning was that someone accessed FBI secure files from your computer at work."

She frowned. "That's what they had?"

"Charity would never be stupid enough to do that," Drew said.

Del nodded. "Agreed. Emma pointed it out more than once and I know she will repeat it Monday. They are in some deep shit too. The bastards should have let us know that there was a chance that our computers had been compromised. By leaving us open like that, who knows who has been screwing around in our system."

That was not good. "Damn."

"Exactly. Tomorrow, if you don't mind, I want you in at work."

"No problem."

"I can come in to help you," Drew said.

"Are you sure?"

He nodded. "You need help to make sure the computers are safe. We might also be able to track back."

Del nodded. "Emma is coming in too."

"Oh, she doesn't have to do that"

Charity knew Emma wasn't delicate, but she hated to drag her into work on the weekend.

"It's an all hands on deck kind of moment, Charity. If I wanted to keep her at home, it wouldn't work. You know how that goes."

"Okay. Tell her I'll text her when we leave so she can meet us there."

Her turned to leave. "Remember, be careful. I doubt Callahan is going to tell anyone what happened tonight before we talk on Monday. Still, we already have them looking at us sideways."

For the first time since they had found out about the investigation, she felt herself crack a little bit. Tears burned the backs of her eyes. She blinked.

"I'm real sorry about this, Del."

He shook his head. "Not your fault. We'll get it all sorted out, Charity."

She nodded.

"Take it easy, Tyson," Del said to Drew before he stepped out of the room and shut the door.

She turned to face Drew. It was the first time she noticed his bruised knuckles.

She grabbed the peas and gave them to him. "Here."

He pressed them to his hand.

"You really didn't need to hit him."

He looked up at her. "I'm sorry. I fucked up."

She sighed and picked up Luke, setting him on the floor before sitting beside Drew on the couch. She slipped her arm over his shoulders.

"Thanks for defending me."

"You're welcome."

They sat that way for a few moments.

"I guess we should go to bed since we have to work tomorrow."

She nodded. "First, I want some chocolate and a hot bath."

"Don't worry, Charity. We'll figure it all out, and things will go back to normal."

She nodded, but she wasn't sure just what normal was for her.

By noon on Saturday, Charity was convinced that they were never going to find out who had hacked their computers.

"Even at the CIA, I've never seen such intricate hacking. This is definitely Foley using me as a set up, but why? How did I come up on his radar?"

Emma shook her head. "I really don't have any idea, Charity. It might be that he wanted something here on the island for some reason, and we were an easy target."

"But to what end?" Drew asked.

Charity rubbed her temples. "Maybe because this is what Foley does. He creates chaos then he does what he wants. So while TJ is playing around with Task Force Hawaii, Foley is doing something else."

"And using you to get at TJ, but this feels different. I read over the case files you emailed me last night."

She blinked. "Emma, I didn't email those until after midnight."

Emma shrugged. "Baby won't settle down, so I'm up a lot. I read them on my tablet in bed."

"Okay, well, what did you find?"

"He doesn't get detected until the last moment. So either there is another reason to reveal you as the target, or the stooge he is using this time used you and is kind of sucky at his job."

"Why Hawaii?" Drew asked.

Emma shook her head. "Not sure, although, the link might be in the FBI."

"I think we're done here, though. All of it loops back to us, and I can't figure it out," Charity said.

"Unless there's a person who broke into TFH offices," Drew suggested. "But we would have known that, right?"

Charity blinked. "Oh, damn." She opened up file menu and started scanning the files. Then, she saw it.

Money Wash.

"Son of a bitch," she murmured.

Emma leaned over her shoulder. "That's the name of the last operation to take down Foley. The one where it all got screwed up."

"And it's on my computer. That's what he did. Remote access. I want to find the bastard and make him cry."

Charity moved her cursor closer to the file wanting to contain it, but Emma stopped her.

"No. He'll know if we do anything."

"But he could access it again."

"I can set up a program to trace it if he does, but I have a feeling he's done. Setting you up was the main reason."

"Dammit. Okay."

Emma tapped her shoulder. "Move over and I'll work on it."

Charity did as she asked and grabbed her coffee cup, realizing it was empty.

"Hey, I'll get you some more. Anyone hungry? I can grab something to munch on. The coffee stand has sandwiches."

"I'm always hungry these days. One for me and some water."

"Thanks, Drew."

He hurried out of the lab, and Charity sat down in the chair he'd vacated.

"He looks better," Emma said as she continued to tap on the keys.

"Yeah. That's one good thing that came out of this."

Emma glanced at her over the computer screen. "Don't worry, Charity. It'll all work out."

She smiled and nodded. In the end, she would be vindicated. If Emma Delano had been on Foley's case from the beginning, Foley would be in jail. Charity knew her professional reputation was in good hands. She was safe in that quarter.

Unfortunately, she was pretty sure her heart was definitely going to be left bruised in the end.

Constant Craving

TJ took a long drink from his bottle of water, then wiped the sweat away from his forehead using his forearm. It was noon, and he'd been working since the sun had peeked over the water. He'd had no sleep the night before, and his jaw hurt like a mother fucker. And he wanted to be pissed.

But he wasn't. He was mad. Mad at Drew for the sucker punch. Irritated that Charity had figured out what was going on, and that Del had ordered him to TFH headquarters on Monday. He was maddest with himself though.

It had been awhile since a woman had captured his attention. Charity was a woman of hidden depths. She was a science nerd, a comic book/sci fi geek, and she was rated an expert shot by the CIA. Add in that she was sweet and sexy, and when he made her smile, he felt as if he owned the world...

He sighed. He looked around the kitchen, happy that he would be done with it this week. It had given him something to concentrate on this weekend instead of Charity. He had called her a couple of times, but she hadn't answered. He didn't blame her, but it didn't mean he would quit trying any time soon.

TJ knew that he was at fault, but he saw no other way around it. He had a job to do, and he doubted that any of them would have done differently. Hell, he had heard the stories about TFH and some of the things they had pulled to get the case done. Still, it didn't make him feel any better.

What kind of cosmic joke was the universe playing on him? Or was it that she seemed out of reach that he wanted her? The moment he thought of it, the image of her smiling at him popped into his head. He closed his eyes and tried to ignore the way heat beat through his blood. The taste of her mouth against his, the way she had sighed and leaned closer...

Nope, it had nothing to do with the job.

His phone rang, and he saw it was his brother Luke.

He could ignore it, but if he did, Luke would tell his mother. Then there would be more calls.

"Hey, loser."

"Nice way to answer the phone, bro."

"What's up?"

"Mom said you had a date the other night."

He frowned. "And? You know I'm not one for kissing and telling."

There was a beat of silence. "Listen, TJ, I understand what went down in DC a year ago, but when you took that job, Mom freaked. We—"

"We?"

"Me, Matt, and Wade. We convinced her you were starting over. Getting a fresh start and going back to what you liked doing."

"Yeah?" The fact that his little brothers were discussing his love life with their mother was embarrassing. Damn.

"But, after a year there and you hadn't had a date...we all started to worry."

"You guys never talked about my love life before."

Luke chuckled. "Actually, we did because you did have a rep in high school. You know how hard that was to live up to?"

"Aw, poor baby boys."

"Fuck you," he said with little heat.

"I had a date. You can quit worrying."

"How did it go?"

"Good." That much was true. That is, until she realized he was investigating her and her roommate punched him. "She has a cat with your name."

"Bullshit."

He chuckled. "Telling you the truth."

"Seriously?"

"Yeah. Even has a female cat named Jess."

"No way. You found a geek?"

"A gorgeous one at that."

"Is she a local?"

"Actually, no. Well, she lives here but she's not originally from Hawaii. Works for a task force here on the islands, but she's originally from Atlanta. And, she has ordered things from Mom and Dad's store."

His brother grunted. "Okay, that is really weird."

"Small world indeed."

"When are you going to tell me her name?"

"It will be on the invitation."

There was a beat of silence, and TJ laughed. He had definitely stunned his little brother, which was never easy. Luke was known for his antics from the time he could crawl, according to his mother.

"I'm not giving you her name. You idiots will look her up on the database, and I don't want that."

One of them would definitely look her up and they would all go through her background. It was already bad enough with his FUBAR of the situation.

"At least I can report I tried. So, are you at the beach today?"

"Nope. Working on the house. Getting the cabinets done

so I can get the appliances and counter tops installed next weekend."

"Sad, bro."

TJ walked to the window and looked out over the rooftops to the little speck of ocean he could see. "I have to get this place ready for family visits. As it is, this is the last of the big stuff I have to do. This time next week, it will be ready for Mom to come bake me cherry pie."

"Oh yeah," his brother said smacking his lips. "I had some last weekend."

"Bastard."

"Ha. Well, I did my job. I have my real job to handle today."

"What are you working on?"

"I'm digging into a cold case. It might have some ties to one that landed on my desk last week."

Luke worked on the Unsolved Crimes Investigation Program with the Texas Rangers. He'd always been someone who loved old mysteries.

"Oh, and you give me shit? Give me a break. You're working weekends. At least I can head down to the beach for a sunset."

He laughed. "Too true. Gotta go. Be sure to call Mom once a week. Otherwise, I have to listen to her complain about not hearing from her poor baby. It makes all of us so ill we have to call in sick to work."

"Aw, sorry you aren't her favorite, but you know, being first does make me that."

"Get bent. Later, bro."

After hanging up with his brother, he felt lighter. He hadn't always had this kind of relationship with his younger siblings. There was four years' difference between him and Luke. His younger brothers had all been born about eighteen months apart, so they were always closer than he had been. Now that they all had a few years under their belts at the Rangers, he had started to talk to them more. Not so much as an older brother, but as a friend. It was the one thing that he liked about his move from DC to Hawaii. He had started to understand how much he really liked and admired his brothers.

With a sigh, he realized none of them would admire him for what he had been playing at here. His mother would definitely box his ears. He grabbed some fresh water and went in search of his doorknobs. He had just a little bit more work to do, and then he would definitely head out to the beach.

The sun was barely peeking over the horizon when Charity's phone rang Monday morning. Unfortunately, she'd been awake for hours. First, a late night call from ADA Deason telling her that they had made a deal with the defendant in the case, so she was off the hook for court Monday. She had almost forgotten about it with everything that had happened on Friday, but she definitely sent her thanks to the man upstairs for this blessing. She would be a wreck today.

When she saw her mother's number, she wanted to ignore it. Her mother had a weird sixth sense about her. She always seemed to call when things sucked, and she could always tell something was bothering Charity.

Ignoring the phone call wouldn't work. Her mother would just call Drew, who was still being an ass. He would rat her out. If she wanted to keep her parents out of it, at least, until they knew just what the hell is going on.

She clicked to answer.

"Hey, Mama."

"Good morning."

"What are you doing calling me so early?"

"I just talked to Drew to find out your schedule because I needed to talk to you, and he said you weren't having a good time of it."

Plans to kill her roommate were back on. It was bad enough he screwed everything up the other night, but ratting her out to her mother was a grave sin.

"I had a long week, but it is looking up. I'm avoiding court because the defendant made a deal. Was there anything you needed?"

Her mother hesitated, and for a second or two, Charity was worried her mother was going to try and coax what was wrong out of her.

"I just had an interesting morning, and well, I can't say anything to your father yet."

"I told you he knows about you and the pool boy."

"Ha ha. I don't know how I raised such a smart ass."

"Better than a dumb one."

"True." Then her mother paused again, and Charity was really starting to worry.

"Mom, is there something wrong?"

"I went to see your grandfather today."

"Grandpa's okay, isn't he?"

"Oh, yes, he is fine. It's just that he had a guest."

She smiled. Her grandfather had been widowed when Charity was just a little girl. He was a charismatic man, who

Constant Craving

could charm just about anyone he came into contact with him, so it was no surprise he had a woman.

"And? I never thought you were a prude."

"I am not being a prude. It was his choice of companion that bothered me."

"Was it a man?"

"Good lord, no. Although, that would have been surprising, but not as upsetting."

"*Mom.*"

"Your grandmother was there."

At first, her brain didn't compute the answer. "What?"

"Your grandmother was there, and not just stopping by. She was wearing a robe."

"You mean Grandma Edwards? Dad's mom. *That* grandmom?"

"That's the only grandma you have."

"They hate each other."

"Yeah."

"I mean; I remember her telling him he had the manners of a dog. A dead dog at that, and I never really understood that expression. How does a dead dog have manners?"

"Your grandmother doesn't always make sense when she's upset. And that day had been bad."

The memory was fuzzy, but she was sure it had something to do with her birthday party. There had been an argument over something she couldn't remember. She was seven and there was yelling and cake thrown. That was all she could remember about the day.

"It is hard for me to even remember if there was a time that they would even say something nice, let alone get busy with each other."

"There is a thin line between love and hate. I just don't know how I am going to tell your father."

"Why do you have to tell him?"

"He has to know. If I don't tell him, then he finds out I knew, he will be extremely pissed."

She opened her mouth, but her mother said, "Damn, there he is now. Nothing to your father about this."

Then she hung up. Charity looked at her phone, then clicked it off.

"What the hell is happening to my life?"

There was a knock at the door.

"Go away."

Drew ignored her and opened the door. "Hey, is everything okay with your family?"

"No. Well, yes. I mean nothing bad, but apparently my grandparents are sleeping together."

Drew blinked. "You mean the conservative uppity white woman and the former Black Panther?"

She closed her eyes. "God, my life sucks."

"At least you don't have court."

"Yeah, at least there is that."

"How about we go get breakfast before going in?"

She opened her eyes and focused on him finally, and realized he was dressed for work.

"Are you planning on going back in?"

"Yeah. I figured I need to get back into work."

"You know Cat's back from Maui, right?"

He nodded. "No worries. I'm going to have to face it sooner or later. Both of us will."

"Give me thirty minutes, twenty-five if you go make me some coffee."

"Got it, Ebony Queen."

When he left, she couldn't fight the smile. It might be a crappy day, and she might not be happy with the outcome, or how stupid she had been, but having Drew up and moving around—dressed even—well, that was definitely a fantastic way to start a Monday.

Chapter Nine

TJ sat at the long table in TFH's conference area and waited. The entire team—even Drew, who had dragged himself into the office—stared at him as if they were each trying to figure out how to torture and murder him. Even a newcomer was giving him the stink eye, an athletic Hawaiian woman he knew was Cat Kalakau. He hadn't been introduced, but she had sniffed in his direction. He had read her file, and he was pretty sure she was configuring the best way to kill him and hide his body. If there was one woman on the team who could do it, it would be her.

Ten minutes earlier, he had arrived. No refreshments had been offered, and Del had been the only one who spoke to him. He was told to sit down before Del and Charity had walked off to Del's office to talk. And that was the last anyone had said a word to him.

He didn't try to engage. There was no need for small talk, as he knew for a fact most of them wanted to rip off his face. He had been in this position before when he ferreted out someone who had been selling data info. Jacob had worked in his office, but it didn't make it any less of a crime because of that. Still, the people he'd worked with for years had turned on him. It was what drove him to the undercover assignment with Remington in the first place.

The door opened, pulling him out of his dark reflections. Del waited to allow Charity to step in front of him. The woman had dressed to kill him, he was sure. The white dress looked simple in design, but the way it hugged her curves made his fingers itch. How did she even walk on those four-inch heels? She made it look so easy, swaying with each step. He wanted to follow those same curves with his hands, his mouth...

He pushed those thoughts aside. He didn't need to be sitting at the conference table with a hard-on. It wasn't like he had much of a chance for relief any time soon. This was about winning them back to work with him. As she walked to her chair, she didn't look at him, but he held his own and didn't beg. Barely.

"So," Del said, taking a seat. Charity sat next to Del and continued to avoid eye contact. "We've been looking at the issues that brought you to us, and we kind of understand why you came in under cover. But now we have a little problem on our hands."

"What?"

Del looked at Emma who took control of the conversation. "Listen, we get that you apparently have cleared her, but the FBI still hasn't. Worse, you've now made her a target."

He glanced at Charity, who had no expression on her face.

"What?"

Constant Craving

No answer from Charity, so Emma continued. "I'm sure you were led here by whatever hacker Foley has been using. But the heart of the matter is that by showing interest, you have made her a target. We know what happened last time you went after Foley."

Dammit. "And how would you know about that?"

"I have my ways. And, well, Del has contacts. The woman you all were shadowing got killed."

He nodded. "But we had no contact with her."

She looked at Del, then back at TJ. "Are you just being obtuse? Foley picks a person and uses them. Now, either he decided to set up Charity for some reason, or the person he is working with did. Either way, you've exposed her. Foley, or his idiot for the moment, will know it is only a matter of time before you clear her. She is a target. He will do anything he can to pin this on her."

"And that means he might kill her." This came from Drew.

"I don't think..." He shook his head. To make sure she couldn't defend herself, there was a very good chance someone would go to the extremes. Not knowing their adversary well enough left them in the dark. They had no way of predicting the person's reactions, even if it was Foley. "Shit."

"Exactly," Del said. "We don't think it is a high possibility, but you have exposed her. Why can't you clear her with the FBI?"

"I'm waiting on security camera footage from LAX."

Charity blinked, and she finally looked at him. "Oh, you mean last month? I flew there to see my folks. Dad had business in LA for a few days, and it had been a few months since I had seen them."

He nodded. "But you are an experienced hacker. You could have faked that whole thing, and I know the FBI is going to need some real proof. I expect to get the warrant today, and we should have what we need by tomorrow."

"Good. Now, I want you working with my team."

For a second, he said nothing. This wasn't going to be kosher with Remington, he knew that much. Remington was old FBI. He didn't like interdepartmental cooperation, because Remington was convinced the entire federal government was corrupt. But, he didn't really have a choice if he wanted to keep close to Charity. Part of that was personal. He wasn't giving up on his chances with her, not by a long shot. Plus, as little as he knew about Foley, he knew a hell of a lot more than TFH did.

"Okay. But we have to be careful about it. The FBI isn't going to like it, and we need to keep it under wraps."

"We're not the ones who left a trail," Emma pointed out.

"And we are not the ones who dated his subject," Charity said.

"I pointed this out the other night, but you asked me out."

All the heads swung down the table to look at her. He detected a fine flush of heat to her face.

"*After* you asked me to coffee. And then you pursued it."

All the heads swung back in his direction.

"After I figured out you were innocent."

She said nothing to that, but the look on her face suggested she thought he was lying.

"Either way, we need to get a lid on this. I want to go over some things with you and Adam," Del said.

He nodded as the rest of the team seemed to know what that meant. They all stood and made their way out of the room. Drew gave him one last look of disdain, before he slipped his arm over Charity's shoulders and walked away with her. TJ watched them until they disappeared around the corner where the elevators were located.

"Come on, Callahan," Del said. "You can fix it later."

He stood and followed both Del and Adam into the commander's office. After closing the door behind him, he took the only other open seat.

"You definitely fucked this one up, Callahan," Del said.

He wanted to argue with him, but TJ knew Del was right.

"True, but it is kind of a trademark of the FBI."

He smiled and leaned back in his chair. "I've been thinking that we're going to need to get Drew out of her apartment."

"That was on my mind too," TJ murmured.

Adam laughed. "He means to get him out of harm's way. He's still not completely out of the woods."

He frowned. "He looks okay to me."

Adam nodded. "He's doing well but the doc said that it would be at least a year before he can be considered fully recovered."

"So, what do you want from me?" he asked.

"I want to go over everything you know about this Foley guy, and I want to know about your boss."

"Tsu?"

Del shook his head. "No. The DC asshole who thought it was a good idea to send you in here to investigate my team. Then, we'll start working on some ideas."

"Anything you need; I'll help if I can."

Del nodded. "You know that helping us isn't going to get you back into Charity's good graces."

"I'm doing it because of the exact reason your wife pointed out. It isn't about getting her back."

Del shared a look with his second-in-command, then looked at TJ. "Of course not. But just a word of advice. Learn how to grovel. You're going to do a lot of it to get her back."

As Del started going over what they knew of the situation, TJ started to understand the enormity of his fuck up and just how hard it was going to be to get Charity back—as Del said.

But one way or another, he was going to do just that.

Half an hour later, Charity found herself irritated that she couldn't concentrate. She needed to write up some reports and go over some of her other findings, but her brain just would not concentrate.

Another fault to lie at the feet of Agent TJ Callahan. Jerk.

So, when Cat came striding in, Charity welcomed the interruption.

"I can hurt him for you," she offered in a calm voice.

"Drew already punched him for me," she said.

Cat offered her a small smile. "I heard about that."

"Have you talked to him?"

"The fed? Why would I talk to that jerk?"

"The fed has a name, and it is TJ. But no. Drew. Have you talked to him?"

Cat sighed and sat down in the chair. "He wants to

pretend there's nothing wrong. I fucked up after he got shot. I felt responsible and guilty."

"But you weren't."

Cat looked out into the lab and shook her head. "I sent him in for a file. If he hadn't come here, he wouldn't have gotten shot."

"And maybe Elle would be dead."

Cat sighed again, this one sounded even lonelier than the first. "That's true. But he's still mad at me."

"He's a little mad at the world, truth be told, but I think the one thing I can thank TJ for is that Drew seems to be making a comeback. He's here today because of the situation."

"At least that's something." Cat looked back at Charity. "Did you really ask him out?"

She crossed her arms. "I can't believe he used that defense. It's just rude."

"You didn't answer me."

"Yes, just as I said. He asked me for coffee, I had to meet with Deason, so I couldn't. Then I suggested we go out."

Cat smiled and it was good to see. "You crack me up."

"I'm glad I make your day so wonderful," Charity said, not bothering to hide sarcasm.

"I'd say that I don't trust him, but I watched him watch you today, Charity. He definitely has a thing for you."

Yes, she had felt his study as she walked out into the conference area. It had made her mad at the time. And really hot. Really, really hot. And that was the sad part about it. Even knowing everything, she still wanted him.

She was what Hawaiians called *pupule*—crazy.

"You know how I feel about lying."

Cat shrugged. "He left stuff out. Not really lying."

"You're supposed to be on *my* side," Charity said, and even to her own ears it sounded childish.

"I am on your side. Doesn't mean we are always going to agree."

"I shouldn't even be attracted to him anymore."

"The heart wants what the heart wants."

"That doesn't sound like you."

Cat laughed. "My grandmother. It's one of her favorite sayings."

The elevator dinged and then steps sounded down the hallway. She knew even before she saw him, it was TJ.

"You might want to cut him some slack," Cat said then rose out of her seat as TJ approached the office.

"Hey. I'm Cat."

"I figured."

"And you have a file on me."

At least he had the ability to look embarrassed. His cheeks flushed and his ears turned red. Damn, that was too cute to ignore.

"I don't mean to run you off if you have work to do."

"I actually have a meeting I need to get to," Cat said as she started out of the office.

"What meeting?" Charity asked.

"We have that terrorism task force thing with the bigwigs from the bases, and Tamilya will be over."

"Tamilya Lowe?"

"Yes," Cat said.

"We went to Quantico together."

"Yeah, we know. I gotta go hunt up Marcus and get over there."

"She's having a meeting with Marcus?" TJ asked.

Cat nodded.

"I didn't think those two would work together again."

"What do you mean?" Charity asked.

He looked between the women. "Well, they were an item back in the day. Dated heavily for a few months."

Cat's eyebrows raised and she looked at Charity. "Did you know that?"

"Yeah."

"And you didn't share that with the rest of us?"

"You just got back from Maui."

Cat frowned. "That will change some of the...discussion."

What Cat meant was that some of the bets they were running on the Tamilya/Marcus romance would be changed.

"Yeah. Talk to Emma about it. She's the one in charge of the funding."

Cat nodded. "See ya later."

When they were alone, the silence was almost deafening. Only the hum of her machines were heard. He said nothing.

"And you are here for what reason?"

He frowned at that and sat—without asking—in the chair Cat had vacated. She sniffed in his direction.

"You can get huffy, and you can get over it."

His voice was as hard as his expression. It was so out of character for him, she blinked.

"What?"

"Listen, I understand you're pissed at me, and I don't blame you. But I'm one of the best experts on Foley. I know more about him than anyone but Remington. You know about him, and you understand hacking."

"Not as well as Emma."

"You don't scare me as much as she does."

She snorted and tried not to be amused. He wasn't stupid, that was for sure.

"We need to work on this together because there's some reason he targeted you."

"Don't blame me. I had nothing to do with it."

He said nothing for a moment. His lips thinned and his jaw flexed. She had the feeling he was trying to keep his temper. That is, if he had one. He had kept his cool, even after Drew punched him.

"I know you have nothing to do with it."

Every word was bit out as if he were barely holding his temper in check. Interesting. She had always been a woman who liked to push things to the extremes.

"So, what are you doing here?"

"Del said we needed to work together, and I wanted to talk this over with you."

"Oh, so that means you'll ask me on a date."

He stared at her a long second. "As I pointed out, you asked me on a date first."

"That should have been a sign."

"A sign of what?"

"That you couldn't take the initiative."

Something flashed hot in his eyes. Those gray eyes were always cool, without any storms. But at the moment, he looked furious. His expression was calm, but his eyes...

"Is that a fact?" he asked, his voice dipped an octave and turned just a little lethal. The sound of it skimmed over her nerves.

As usual, she ignored his tone. When she was hurt, she could definitely wound back. She nodded and leaned back in her chair. She tried her best to look relaxed. She would not let him know how upset she was.

"You didn't really go after me, because it was all about the job."

"That's what you think?"

She shrugged.

"If it was about the job, I would have had you in bed easily."

Her stomach quivered at the way his voice had dipped deeper, adding an edge of danger to it. This was not the fun geek she had discussed the Marvel Universe with, and argued about the finer qualities of David Tennant. This was Agent Callahan. Cold. Calculating. Sexy.

"I highly doubt that."

But even she heard the shaking in her voice. The smile curving his lips was not the flirty one she was used to. He looked as if he was the cat who ate the proverbial canary. He rose to his feet, all the while not breaking eye contact with her.

"Come on, Charity. You know better than that. You and I both know that you wanted it as much as I did."

His voice had turned silky, seductive, but not anything she had heard before. This was a very dangerous man.

She shook her head and fought the urge to back up around the desk. He came around to stand in front of her, each step taken with a kind of lethal grace that she would have attributed to a panther. A predator.

He leaned down and placed his hands on the arms of her chair.

"I might have come here to investigate, but at least I have been honest about my feelings." He leaned closer and she couldn't move. She didn't want to. The heat of him, the smell of his flesh…it was just as intoxicating as it had ever been.

He nuzzled her neck, and she felt the brush of his lips, then teeth and tongue. Heat flared hotter, her head started to spin. Damn, her nipples were hard against her bra.

She felt herself leaning closer, wanting the warmth of his body, needing to touch, to taste. She closed her eyes and did just that. She almost fell out of the chair, as he pulled away. She gained her balance and shot him a dirty look.

"What was that for?"

"To show you that I could have had you if I wanted to. But I held back."

"Oh, well, that makes me like you even more."

She rose to her feet. She couldn't look at him because she was embarrassed to admit he was right. If he had wanted her Monday night, she wasn't sure she would have refused. She didn't jump in the sack with just anyone, but from the moment she had seen him, she had felt a connection.

Then she felt him behind her. The warmth against her body again. This time, the tender kisses on her neck seemed innocent, but they made her even hotter.

"Sorry," he whispered against her neck. "I have a temper but I rarely lose it."

"You call that losing your temper?"

"I…I disrespected you."

Of course, he wasn't trying to seduce her. It was still part of the job. Her shoulders sagged.

"Now what did I say?"

"Nothing. Just, give me some time this morning then we can talk this afternoon."

He turned her around. "I will if you will tell me what is wrong."

She looked up at him, then away. It was pathetic that she still wanted him, even though she knew what he did to her. "It's nothing really. Just go back to work."

"No." He slipped a finger beneath her chin and urged her to look up at him again. "I want to know what is bothering you."

"I'm never good if I am not working on an equal basis with a man. In a relationship I mean. I can't seem to control myself around you, even after what you did to me."

He shook his head. "Do you know the entire time I worked on the Foley case last time, I wasn't found out? At least until the very end. I didn't last a week with you. And from the moment I met you, I was trying to figure out a way to clear your name. You're a good woman, Charity, that is part of the reason."

"What's the other part?" she asked when he didn't continue.

"It took every bit of my control to leave your apartment Monday night. Hell, right now I'm trying to figure out if there is some available flat surface I can use to seduce you."

She opened her mouth to respond, but snapped it shut. It took her a moment to compose herself. "You are not."

He nodded. "I am." He brushed his mouth against hers and she felt it all the way to her toes. "I screwed up, but I *will* prove myself to you."

"TJ." She couldn't think of anything else to say.

"I do plan on having you, Charity Edwards."

She shivered against him, as she heard the ding of the

elevator. TJ kissed her forehead then released her as he stepped back.

"Hey," Emma said as she walked in, her husband a shadow behind her. "I think we might have something here on the islands."

"What?"

"I have the information we found out this weekend."

TJ looked at Charity, then back at Emma. "What did you find?"

"Our servers were hacked around the time of the breach. I followed the worm that was sent to your email, and figured out that it was sent from an HPD memo that was sent everywhere. Yours, though, seems to be the only one that downloaded the file. It might be Foley, but it is definitely whoever is working for him."

"I thought they had some ID on the guy?" Del asked.

"No pictures if that is what you mean. They did lift a partial off a rental car one of his victims had used. It didn't belong to the victim or anyone from the rental agency. They are pretty sure it is from Foley."

"And the name?"

TJ nodded. "The alias he used the most often. But I still can't understand why he would use TFH."

"Maybe it's his accomplice," Charity said.

"But it would have to probably be someone familiar with the set up."

"Why do you say that?" Del asked.

"TFH is big here, and it's getting some notice on the mainland. Still, it isn't as well known as some of the others."

"But you said that there was a thought that Foley had

some federal connections, right? Feds definitely know about us," Charity said.

Del looked at Charity. "I want to put some protection on you."

She frowned. "I don't need it with Drew there."

"That's the other thing. I would rather Drew move out for right now."

"What?"

"You have a target on you, and while it isn't a big one, we can't risk his health. And we have to make him think that it is to help you."

She frowned. "I get that, but I don't know if I like it."

"He isn't going to like it," Emma said.

"He can just get used to it," TJ said.

Emma smiled. "I had a feeling that was going to be your response. I think we can work it out though. Our condo is empty for a few months, and I need someone there. It's always good to have someone living there, you know. We'll guilt him into it."

"Yeah, he'll do it if he thinks that you and the boss need the help. I don't know about a security detail. If I am being watched, we need to make sure it looks normal. Having a black and white, or one of the TFH folks out there is going to draw attention. The building has a good security system."

"I'll be staying there."

All three of them turned their attention to TJ.

"I don't think you have a say in this," Charity said.

"I think I do. Besides, I can report back that I am *romancing* you. If we have someone watching dispatches at the FBI, it would work."

"I have to agree with him," Del said. Irritated, she

rounded on him, but he held up his hands. "Listen, I know you aren't happy with it. But you'll have a free room, and no one will know that he is in there. Plus, he can help you keep a lid on any surveillance of the technical kind. We are dealing with a bastard of a hacker—or at least someone who likes to hire them—and we need you two to be careful about phone calls."

As if on cue, her cell rang with her mother's tune. She rolled her eyes.

"Are you going to answer that?" Del asked.

"No. It's my mom. She can wait."

"I'll talk to Drew for you. He will feel sorry for me because of junior," Emma said, brushing her hand over her belly.

"Guilt does work well on him."

"We'll do dinner tonight. Duke's."

She nodded.

"I'll want to talk to you later, Callahan."

TJ nodded, as the couple left them alone.

"Are you having problems at home?"

She glanced at him. "You mean with Drew? No, he'll move for Emma."

"No. Your mom."

"Oh, the phone call? No, not much. Not really."

"I guess I need to talk to Del. What time do you think you'll be at your apartment tonight?"

She studied him for a long moment, then she said, "Why don't you come to dinner with us?"

The lines of his face softened, and she tried to fight the need to soothe him. "You really want me to come?"

She heard the need, the desire to be with her. It gave her

heart a bit of a jolt but she crushed the hopeful ping. She did not need to be romanced by the agent. They needed to solve the case and get him out of her hair.

"Yes, but it will also give us an excuse."

"And excuse for what?"

"For whomever might be watching me."

"Is that all?"

"Yes."

But even to her own ears, it did not ring true. His mouth curved, telling her that he knew she was fibbing. "Okay. You got it. I'll pick you up."

She shook her head. "I'll just grab a ride."

It was his turn to deny her. "No. It's a date. I pick my dates up." He leaned forward and brushed his mouth over hers.

"What was that for?"

"Down payment."

Then, before she could smack him, he left. She wanted to deny him, but her body was still humming with need. It had been a long time since a man had messed her up so much—if ever. Her phone started ringing again, and she knew this time, her mother would not wait. She pushed thoughts of TJ away and answered. It was enough to deal with this right now.

Chapter Ten

Charity rushed through her apartment tidying up. It figured the day she needed to be home and ready to take on a challenge, her phone rang off the hook at work. The result was that she had hit traffic on the way home. Even as close as she lived to work, things had moved a snail's pace. Half way home, she had realized it would have been faster to walk than drive.

After she changed the sheets on the guest bed, she changed into a comfortable Hawaiian dress. After freshening up, she did one last check of her bedroom. Charity heard the doorbell just as she stepped out of her bedroom. Jess and Luke followed her. She wanted to be dressed and ready to leave as soon as TJ arrived. She had achieved that, but she was flustered and didn't want him to know.

Drawing in a deep breath, she counted backwards from ten. When she felt she had calmed down enough, she walked to the door, her sandals in her hand. Opening it up, the first thing she noticed was the bags. He had a backpack and two duffle bags. Then, the way he was dressed. Her gaze traveled up, over his tanned legs to the black shorts and then the black and gold Hawaiian shirt.

"What?" he asked.

She shook her head and stepped back. "Come on in."

He did as she requested.

"That looks like a lot of stuff."

"I didn't want to keep running out to Waimanalo every day for clothes."

She said nothing as they stood there. The moment stretched out and awkwardness set in. The situation was odd enough. He was practically moving in with her. Other than Drew, she had never lived with a man outside of family members. And while it was just for the case, Charity felt as if the world was shifting beneath her feet. She had lost control of her life.

"Where does this go?" he asked holding up his duffle bag.

She blinked at him, then looked at the bag. "What?"

He frowned. "Are you feeling okay?"

Mentally, she shook herself out of her stupor. "Sorry. Yeah, this way."

She led him to the room Drew had occupied just a few hours earlier. Her friend hadn't been happy with the arrangement, but he understood. Luke and Jess, not so much. Her cats had meowed their displeasure, and had tried to make off in Drew's bag. In the end, when they had been left with only Charity, they had given her a look of disdain, before disappearing back into the guest room. Traitors.

"Here you go," she said, stepping aside and letting him enter the room. "Living in one room will probably not be as nice as a house."

He shrugged. "The kitchen at the house won't be done

for a couple of weeks, so cooking on a hot plate or grilling is the only way. Nice to be able to nuke something in the microwave."

He set is bag on the bed. Luke and Jess easily jumped on the bed to inspect the new item. TJ turned to face Charity.

"Are we going to talk about this?" he asked.

"I can't."

"We need to."

She wasn't ready for this. She crossed her arms beneath her breasts and cocked her head to the side. "Isn't that the woman's line?"

"First, that's damned sexist. And second, it'll just fester and get worse."

"So, now our relationship, what little there is, is like a rotting, oozing wound?"

"You're being deliberately obtuse."

She shrugged. "I just want to make sure we are clear where we stand and how we both view the relationship."

"I think I made my views on our relationship clear earlier in your office."

She fought the shiver that wanted to run through her body. She had pushed the memory to the back of her mind and tried to work all day. Unfortunately, thoughts of his mouth on her flesh, the way his heat had surrounded her had plagued her throughout the day. If she could, she would take some leave and go see her family, or go to Vegas with some friends. She needed something to work him out of her system and make her sane again.

"We have too much on our plates right now, TJ."

He opened his mouth to respond, but her phone went off. She glanced down.

"We have to go. Most of them are already there."

He didn't look happy about it, but he nodded. "We will finish this discussion someday, Charity."

"I consider it done now."

He shook his head. "Not by a long shot."

As the sun started to dip below the horizon, TJ found himself sitting at a table with the TFH team. It was an odd experience, to say the least. Half of the table were still giving him the evil eye, and the other half seemed to be reserving judgment. And then there was Drew, who was openly hostile to TJ. From the moment he arrived, Drew had been ready with the barbs. First, he attacked the FBI, and then he made disparaging remarks about Texas.

TJ really didn't give a fuck. What he cared about was sitting next to him. *Who* would be the better term. She was all that is important to him now. Clearing her name and setting things right. Then, he would work on *them*.

He used the case to get into her apartment. He should feel ashamed, but he wasn't. A man had to do what he needed to do to win a woman's affections. If that meant sleeping in the room next to hers with a case of the blue balls, then that was what he would do.

He sipped his water and winced. The noise level was starting to get to TJ. They were not a quiet bunch that was for sure. He understood family dinners, and that was definitely what this was. They all interacted as he did with his brothers and parents.

They had a long table, which took up most of the back of

the restaurant. Delano sat at the head of the table, which made sense, since he was the patriarch. Emma sat on his right and Adam, who didn't look like he wanted to be there, was on the left.

Emma leaned over and, not too quietly, asked Charity, "What is the fed doing here?"

Charity shrugged. "I figured it was better that he was close to keep an eye on him."

"Do you always talk about people in front of them as if they weren't there?" he asked.

"Take it as a good sign, Callahan," Delano said. "When they are talking behind your back, they are betting on you."

"Betting?"

Emma shot her husband a dirty look. "Don't say anything about that to the fed. He could arrest us."

"I'm not looking to arrest anyone."

"Not now," Drew said.

"Drew, behave," Charity said, with no menace in her voice.

Drew's features softened. "I still don't get why we are letting him get away with it."

TJ opened his mouth to defend himself, but Charity intervened. "We never said he got away with anything."

The warning in her tone had TJ swinging his attention to her. Her gaze did not move from his, as she sipped her Cosmo. Oh, it was an evil smile, that was for sure. The hum of conversation around him seemed to fade away, as she drew her tongue over the rim of the glass, then smacked her lips.

When he made eye contact again, her eyes were sparkling with amusement. She had done that on purpose.

He leaned closer and said, "Watch yourself, Charity."

"Don't worry, Callahan. I know just how to handle myself."

Then, Adam, who was sitting next to TJ, tapped his arm and asked him a question. He did his best to concentrate on the question about his family history with the Texas Rangers, but in the back of his mind, he formulated his next move with Charity.

Charity was feeling pleasantly buzzed by the time their food arrived. She hadn't really been in the mood for a family dinner, but she was glad she had been left with no choice. Del had made sure she had known that before she left work.

She glanced at her companion from the corner of her eye. He had been handling himself just fine. Drew had settled down, and talk had moved onto work. Anyone watching them would assume they were out for the night and TJ was her date.

"You know, you're supposed to eat the food," he said. He had leaned closer and his breath warmed her earlobe.

Before she could think, she turned to face him. It brought them nose to nose.

"I was just enjoying the moment."

His mouth curved. "Is that a fact?"

She nodded.

"You should eat. You had a few drinks."

Normally, she would tell him to mind his own damned business. But, she thought it might be a good idea. She needed something to soak up the alcohol.

Constant Craving

She turned back to her plate and started to eat just as Graeme's voice raised in anger.

"I don't understand how you can be so bloody beautiful and such a pigheaded Sassenach."

"I cannot believe you just said that," Dr. Middleton said.

"Well, what do you expect? When I talked to your father yesterday, I had to say we were waiting. It is the third bloody time he's asked. It's bloody embarrassing."

Elle glanced down the table, and was aware of the audience. She looked back at her lover.

"Can we discuss this later?"

"How much later? Are we going to wait until that child you're carrying is born a bastard?"

There was another beat of silence, then everyone started to congratulate them. But they were overruled by the doctor.

"I told you to wait three months."

"It's been three months."

Elle looked down the table and at the people in the restaurant who were staring at her. Then, she turned her wrath toward her lover.

"You Scottish goat. No. That is an insult to goats. I don't have a word for you. You are the worst."

Elle jumped out of her seat and hurried away. McGregor got up to follow her, but Charity got up.

"Graeme, sit down. She's in the ladies' bathroom."

He gave her a mulish look. "I don't care."

"Well, Elle will, and I can calm her down."

He didn't like it. He was beyond furious with the situation, but it was hard to be mad at the man. He was in love and excited about a baby.

"Okay. But, you have five minutes, then I'm invading."

She smiled and rose to her tiptoes to kiss his cheek. "Congratulations, Daddy."

He smiled. "Thanks. Please, go check on her."

She nodded and made her way to the bathrooms. Charity found Elle standing at the vanity crying.

"Oh, sweetie, what's the matter?" she asked as she stepped up to stand next to the doctor. Charity put her arm around her.

Elle sniffed into a tissue. "That man has the manners of a pig."

Charity chuckled. "Yes, but you knew that before you fell in love with him, so that's on you."

Elle shook her head. "I must be mental."

"Don't tell anyone that. We could have a lot of cases overturned."

Her friend chuckled, but it ended on a sob. It was so out of character for her, Charity was not sure what to do, so she let her friend cry for a little bit.

"So, you're pregnant?" Charity asked after a few minutes.

She nodded. "I lost my first child, and I didn't want anyone to know this time around, not until we passed that magical twelve-week mark."

"And? You turned that big, bad Scot down?"

The door opened and Emma waddled in with Cat behind her.

"So, where are we at?" Emma asked.

"Elle is pregnant. Graeme proposed."

"Well, of course he did. He's in love with you," Cat said.

"I don't want to get married because I'm pregnant."

"Don't. Get married because you love him." This came

from Emma, who said it in a tone that said she thought Elle had lost her mind.

"I do love him."

"There you go," Emma said. "Another wedding and another baby. And now I have to pee. That's what I spend the majority of my time doing these days."

Emma wandered down to the stalls. Elle laughed.

"Sure, be amused. Your day shall come," she called out from behind the locked door.

For the first time since Graeme announced her pregnancy, Elle smiled. "Yeah, it will."

"Now, you need to tell the Scottish goat," Cat said with a laugh.

"I can't believe I called him that."

"I can. He was being one," Charity said.

Emma came out and washed her hands. "Come on. Let's go enjoy the announcement."

The four women made their way out to the dining area.

"So, what's going on with you and the fed?" Emma asked.

"Nothing."

The other three women stopped and turned to face her.

"What?"

"Nothing is going on?" Cat asked. "You looked like you were about to kiss just a few minutes ago."

"You're insane," she said. Even to her own ears, she sounded defensive.

"Sure. Although, he keeps watching everything you do," Cat said with a smirk.

She opened her mouth to refute them, but Emma stopped her. "No more denials. Just tell us something. Are his bags in your guest room or in your room?"

"They are in the guest room."

That she could say without lying. For now. Even though, right now, she was trying to remember why she had him put them there. Because it was the smart thing to do, that's why.

"What a waste. I would have moved him right into my room," Emma said.

"Do you want us to tell Del that?"

"Why would he be offended or threatened by that? It's true. Listen, I messed around with Del and wasted a lot of time. He's hardheaded, so that is the only reason we are together. Thank God. He's the only person who can handle me."

"That was a different situation than mine."

Emma shook her head and looked like she was going to argue, but Charity stopped her.

"No more arguing. Graeme is going to storm back here if we don't get back there. We can argue about my love life later."

Charity watched the numbers illuminate as they rode the elevator up to her floor.

"Do y'all do that a lot?" TJ asked.

She glanced at him just as the door opened. She stepped off the lift before she answered. "Not as often as we would like. Work keeps us busy, and a lot of times plans are cancelled. So, when we get a chance, we take advantage of it."

He nodded as she opened her door. She was feeling really good, she thought. Really, really good. Okay, it might have something to do with the three Cosmos she'd had. She had never been a heavy drinker, and the bartender had been generous with his concoctions.

They both took their shoes off and lined them up against the wall by the door. Jess and Luke made their way out into the living room, rubbing their bodies up against Charity first, then moving onto TJ. Traitors.

Dropping her purse on the breakfast bar, she went to the refrigerator to get a drink of water. She loved her Cosmos, and she loved macadamia nut crusted fish, but with the alcohol consumption, she was feeling parched.

After filling the glass, she turned to face TJ. He was watching her with that look—the one she was sure drove people crazy. A person couldn't read what he was thinking with those flat eyes and the almost blank expression.

"Stop that."

"What?"

"Looking at me that way."

His eyebrows shot up. "What way?"

Oh, his tone told her that he was definitely screwing with her.

"Like I'm a suspect."

He shook his head as she nodded.

"How do you know how I look at suspects?"

Oh, God. His voice. The Texas accent had deepened and rolled over the words. It did all kinds of funny things to her insides.

"I just do. It's like you're trying to figure me out."

"Most of the time, I've already figured out suspects. You...not so much."

Charity frowned, then took another sip of water. He wasn't making all that much sense, but it might not be him. It might just be the drinks with dinner. "What's that supposed to mean?"

He didn't answer for a long time. He stared at her with a look that she imagined most people would term as predatory. "You're a complicated woman."

"I take pride in that."

He acknowledged that with a nod. "I assumed you would."

"Now what is *that* supposed to mean?"

He just smiled. Oh, hell, he looked so cute. His hair was particularly curly today. And that smile—it would entice a nun to sin.

"Charity?"

"What?"

"Sorry. Was just thinking."

"About what?"

"That big bed in your bedroom."

"TJ." His name escaped on a sigh that sounded more like a plea. After the chat with Emma, she had been thinking of all kinds of things, one of them was how much she wanted TJ. Like wanted him more than she wanted her next breath. It wasn't a feeling she was accustomed to.

"But then, as I said earlier, any flat surface would do for me."

Her pulse scrambled, and the air seemed to back up in her lungs. She shouldn't want a man who had done the things he had done. But what if he was telling her the truth earlier?

"What did you mean about not revealing yourself in your last investigation?"

"It means that when I'm around you, I can't think

straight. Mainly because it's hard to think with no blood in my brain."

He had stepped closer. It was beyond intimate. She could feel the heat of his body. It never failed to get to her.

"I have no problem with my job, keeping it professional, but from the first time I met you, I couldn't seem to be that way. Hell, just seeing your picture for the first time, before I met you, I wanted you. I didn't realize how much until you smiled at me."

He took the glass of water out of her hands and set it on the counter behind her, then he caged her in by placing his hands on either side of her against the counter.

"This isn't a good idea, TJ."

"I disagree," he said, as he nibbled on her bottom lip. "Is it smart? No. But good...actually you might be right."

He said nothing else, as he nuzzled her neck. Oh, God. He brushed his mouth over her pulse point, then his teeth and tongue. The man was driving her crazy.

"So, you agree. Not a good idea."

"No." He worked his way to her earlobe, took it between his teeth, and gave it a tug. His breath was hot against her flesh. As he pressed his body closer, she felt the hard, long length of him against her. "I think it is an *excellent* idea."

Charity said nothing, but she leaned her head away to give him better access. Heat flashed through her as every drop of moisture seemed to dry up. She closed her eyes and moaned.

"Charity?"

She forced herself to open her eyes and look at him. There was no doubting what he was asking. He was leaving it up to her. She knew he would walk away and give her space if she said no, but she didn't want to say no. It was probably stupid and definitely complicated, two things she tried to avoid for the most part, but with TJ, she didn't care.

"Yes."

He groaned and took her mouth in a hot, wet, completely erotic kiss. It flashed through her, pushing her arousal to new heights, and it was just a kiss. He tugged her forward and started walking backwards. As he worked their way through the living room, the rush of the moment hit her. This man, this time. It was right. If it wasn't, she didn't want to know about it. They bumped against the wall, as he tried to undo the tie at the back of her neck for her halter top. Her breasts spilled free of the soft cotton fabric. Going without a bra had probably been the best idea in a long time. With a wiggle, her dress fell to the floor at their feet.

He stopped just inside her doorway and stared. He shot a look up at the ceiling and mouthed the words *thank you*, then he bent his head, taking her nipple into his mouth. Heat seared through her as need rose. She speared her fingers through his hair as he teased her. The man was dangerous with that mouth. He had barely touched her with his hands, and she was ready to explode.

Need coursed through her. They fell onto the bed, with little planning from what she could tell, but she didn't care. She loved the feel of his rough hands working over her flesh.

They both fumbled with his shirt, giggling as they fought to open the buttons. Before he had it off, Charity started to work on his shorts, pulling the zipper down. He batted her hands away.

"Hey," she said, still laughing. "I'm practically naked, and you have too many clothes on."

"Give me a second here, woman," he said, frustration easy to hear in his voice.

She laughed, enjoying him, relishing this moment with just him.

He shucked off his shirt, dropping it on the floor with her dress, then he eased them to the bed. Once she was laying on top of her mattress, he slipped her panties off and spread her legs apart. Without hesitation, his mouth was on her, his tongue slipping inside of her slick passage. She was so wet, wetter still as he tasted her. The hum that tore from his throat rushed through her, pushing her over that first peak.

The intensity of it left her shattered, unable to even comprehend what was happening. He rose then, slipping off the rest of his clothes and retrieving a condom out of his wallet. He tore the package open and rolled it on before joining her back on the bed.

He moved between her legs, kneeling on the bed. Taking hold of her by the hips, he thrust into her in one, long movement. As he started to move within her, she moaned. Her orgasm had left her weak, unable to move. But even as she thought it might not happen, the rush of excitement hit her again.

"Yes," TJ said. "Look at me, Charity."

She fought to get her eyes opened and then heat surged again. She could smell the Hawaiian night air on him, and the underlying scent she would always know him by. His fingers bit into her flesh as he increased the rhythm. She arched up, her eyes sliding closed, as the sheer enormity of her next orgasm blew through her. It left her shaking, as she felt him thrust one more time. With a shout, he followed her into pleasure this time.

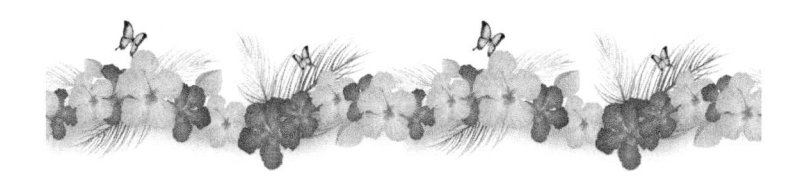

Chapter Eleven

TJ was pretty sure he was dead. The only sign that he was still breathing was the beating of his heart.

"Hey, you weight a ton," Charity said pushing at his shoulder.

He grunted and didn't move. Every muscle in his body seemed to have turned to mush. It would be impossible for him to move. He might just have to stay there the rest of his life.

"TJ?"

He drew in a deep breath, and along with it, her scent. Sweet and pungent at the same time. Even that was complex. The woman had layers and layers to her, and he wasn't sure if he would ever get down to the bottom—but he knew that uncovering them would be interesting.

"There is a reason they call it *dead weight*."

She laughed. Since he was still inside of her, he could feel all the delicious vibrations run from her through him. He was starting to realize her laugh was one of the best sounds in the world.

"Are you saying you're dead?" she asked.

He forced himself to move. With great effort, he rose to his elbows so he could look down at her. Moonlight dappled her skin. Her hair was a tangled mess against the brilliant yellow pillow case, and her mouth curved up in a one-sided smile. Her eyes were closed. Damn, the woman was gorgeous. Physically, that was easy to see, but there was a joy within her. He was sure that was the reason he had become so infatuated with her so easily. She didn't hide her feelings, and she wouldn't lie about them.

"I'm saying I might be. Old man like me, all this activity...plus, add in that I'm fairly certain I saw God once or twice."

Her smile widened as she opened her eyes and slipped her hands up his arms. "Is that a fact?"

He nodded and brushed his mouth against hers. "Yep."

It was barely a touch, but he wanted more. The urge to deepen the kiss, to lose himself in her once more almost overwhelmed him. He didn't understand the driving need he had for her. Well, beyond the obvious sexual desire. There was something about her that drew him in and held onto him. He just didn't understand it.

She pushed at his shoulder again. "I do appreciate that, but I'm serious about the *being heavy* thing."

With regret, he rolled off her. The sigh she released was almost comical.

"I can breathe again."

"I'm not *that* heavy."

Instead of trying to cover her nude body, she stretched, bowing off the bed. He had never met a woman who was so comfortable in her own skin. Damn, was he ever going to get used to her? With a sigh, she settled back down and looked at him.

"What?"

"Nothing, no comments from me, except that I'm glad you're not modest."

"I've never been afraid of nudity. Never bothered me in the least. We traveled a lot when I was young, lots of museums. Plus, my parents had a very healthy view on sexuality. No shaming people for what came natural."

"I, for one, would like to thank them for that."

With a throaty laugh, she raised up to settle her weight on one elbow and looked at him. "Honey, you are all solid muscle. I take it you work out."

"Used to. Working on the house, I don't really have to now."

She smiled as she ran her fingers down his chest. "Yeah, I can see that."

He shook his head and laughed. "You are always surprising me."

"Is that a good thing? I would think it was."

"Yeah," he said, leaning in to kiss her again. He rose from the bed and went to the bathroom to throw away the condom. When he returned, she was propped up on her elbow. The only light in the bedroom came from the bathroom, but he could easily see her. It almost stopped his heart seeing her against the crimson red and gold comforter.

"What?"

"Just trying to figure out how I got so lucky."

She snorted. "You *were* lucky. I mean, after everything you did, and I still let you have me."

He cocked his head. "I would say we both had each other."

For a long moment, she said nothing. Then, her lips curved. "Yeah, I like that."

"And I think we are about to have each other again," he said walking toward the bed.

"You think?"

He climbed onto the mattress and pulled her closer. Easily, slowly, he kissed her. She hummed. The sound of it moved over his flesh and sunk into his soul.

"Yeah," he said, nibbling on her bottom lip. "But this time, I plan on taking my time."

Just before dawn, TJ felt a sharp pain vibrate from his chest through his body. He opened his eyes and found himself face-to-face with Jess. She was sitting on his chest, clawing at it. Her brilliant blue eyes were easy to see in the dark room.

"Go away," he whispered.

The cat stopped for a second and then, without breaking eye contact, she clawed at his chest again.

"Mother fucker," he said, trying to keep his voice low. He didn't want to wake Charity, who was snoring softly next to him. He lifted Jess and set her on the floor. Then, he felt another paw on his back and the scratch that followed.

Another oath slipped from his lips, before he lifted Luke and put him down on the ground next to Jess. He looked over his shoulder at Charity. She was still sleeping, snuggled up with her pillow. He'd had her three times the night before, and still he craved her. He wanted nothing more than to ease her to wake with a kiss, then do even more. But, at this moment, she looked so peaceful, he really didn't want to disturb her. So, he eased away and out of bed. He looked down at the cats, who continued to study him.

"Get used to it. I'm going to be around here a lot."

Jess licked her paw as Luke snarled at him.

"Sorry, bud, but your claim on your mistress is over."

Jess still ignored him, and Luke gave him a look that said he would gladly smother TJ in his sleep. So, apparently, Luke was okay with him being a friend, but not in Charity's bed. The stupid cat better just get used to it. Not wanting to disturb Charity, he decided to go take a shower.

Charity came awake slowly. She knew she was alone in the bed without looking. TJ had been quiet, but Charity had felt him leave the bed just a few moments earlier. With a yawn, she stretched her arms over her head and then winced. Damn, she had used muscles the night before that had been long unused—which was odd for her. From her early twenties, Charity had had an active sex life. She didn't exactly sleep around, but she never shied away from her sexuality. As she had told TJ, her parents had been open, and her mother had insisted that a woman had every right to sexual satisfaction. But...she was sure that TJ had used her body in ways that had never been attempted before. She smiled. Damned if she hadn't enjoyed every minute of it too.

Drawing in a deep breath, she turned over to her side.

The mattress still had his imprint. The sheets smelled of him. She heard the shower and sighed. Maybe she should join him. The master bath shower was big enough for the two of them. She smiled and slipped from the bed, but not before she noticed his phone buzzing. The picture was of the Ryan Reynold's adaption of *Deadpool*. The top of the screen read Wade. She didn't answer, as that was invasion of privacy, but she sat on the bed trying to work through what was bothering her.

Wade was the real name of *Deadpool*. What were his other brothers' names? Luke—and they had laughed at that because of her cat. As in Luke Cage. Matt was the other brother. Matt Murdock who was also known as *Daredevil*.

And that left her with a man who preferred to be called TJ. He was called The Hammer. Both Charity and Emma had looked and could not find his name anywhere. It was as if he had been named with the initials. She worked through all the names of Marvel—since his parents seemed to be leaning that way with the other three. What name would embarrass him enough not to use it?

The moment it struck, she giggled. *No*. Could his parents have been so horrible? And if they had been that horrible, she definitely wanted to meet them both. It was almost too perfect. Charity popped up off the bed and walked into the bathroom. She opened the door and steam poured out. The mirror was clouded. She walked to the shower and slowly opened the door. At first, he didn't seem to notice her. He was rinsing shampoo out of his hair. Damn...she had said it before, and she had been right. The man was built. She saw the injury to his shoulder. She had felt it the night before, but in the harsh light, it looked worse. She let her gaze travel down his body. He glanced over his shoulder at her. The smile he shot her had her heart quivering.

"Morning. I didn't wake you, did I?"

She shook her head. "Do you mind if I join you?"

His mouth curved. "Not at all."

He moved up closer to the shower head, and she stepped in behind him. He was warm and wet and too much to resist. She slipped her arms around his waist and pressed her body against his.

"Hmm," was all he said, but the satisfaction was easy to hear.

"So, Thor, how did you like last night?"

He stilled. "What?"

She laughed and drew back. He turned to face her. "Thor. What does the J stand for?"

He hesitated, and she knew he was trying to come up with a lie. It delighted her even more.

"How did you figure it out?"

"Your brother called. I didn't answer it, of course. I couldn't. But, I saw the pic. Then I thought about your brother's names, the fact that your parents run a comic book store, and there is only one name in the Marvel Universe that would embarrass you enough to go by an acronym. So what *does* the J stand for?"

"Jackson. My mother's maiden name."

She thought about it, then said the name out loud. "Thor Jackson Callahan." A bubble of laughter escaped before she could stop it. "Sorry. It couldn't have been easy running around with that name."

He rolled his eyes. "You have no idea."

"Your secret is safe with me, for now."

He was quiet for a long moment again, then his mouth curved. "Is that a fact?"

She nodded.

"Of course, I could offer some kind of payment for it."

Charity felt the heat in her rise, her body already responding to the dip in his voice. She glanced down. He was fully erect, his cock curving up against his belly.

"Yeah? Like what?"

He stepped closer and slipped his hands around her waist, then down to her ass. Pressing closer, she couldn't fight the hum that vibrated out of her chest. Bending his head, he kissed her. Not a brush of the mouth, but thrusting his tongue into her mouth. She sucked on his tongue.

He groaned against her, then pulled away, falling to his knees in front of her. Looking up at her, he pressed his mouth against her sex, thrusting his tongue inside of her. She moaned as her knees buckled under his sexual onslaught. Before she could stop herself, she was coming, her scream echoing in the shower stall.

With quick movements, he turned off the shower, then dragged her out of the stall. He frowned and turned to leave.

"I have condoms in the draw," she said, dragging it open and grabbing them.

He yanked one from her hands, ripped one open, then rolled it on. Charity needed this, needed the connection she felt when he was inside of her. She stepped closer, but he turned her and bent her over. After situating her hands on the counter in front of her, TJ brushed his hands over her flesh. As he watched her in the mirror, he slipped his fingers down her spine. When he reached her rear end, he broke eye contact to look down as he splayed his hands over both of her cheeks.

"You have the most amazing skin, but this ass."

He sighed before slipping one hand between her legs and into her again. She was still sensitive from her orgasm, but she loved when he added another finger. Her body was already responding again. She closed her eyes. He skimmed one hand up to her breast.

"So, wet," he whispered and bent down to kiss her shoulder.

He drew his fingers out of her and she opened her eyes. She watched him, watching her, as he slipped his fingers into his mouth. He hummed against his fingers. Just that sound almost had her coming.

"You taste so good, Charity."

He positioned himself behind her and placed a hand on each hip. With one hard thrust, he was inside her. She closed her eyes, but he did not like that.

"Look at me, Charity."

It took her a few seconds. He stopped moving. She forced them open the rest of the way. As TJ started to move again, his fingers dug into her flesh. He seemed to go deeper, harder each time. All the while, he kept eye contact in the mirror.

It was the most erotic experience of her life.

His rhythm increased, and he slid a hand down to her clit. He teased it as he continued to thrust. It didn't take her long to go up and over again. She closed her eyes and let herself go. But that wasn't enough. TJ leaned down, kissing her neck.

"Again" he ordered. Charity didn't think she would be able to do it again, but his talented fingers and cock had her soaring once more. This time, he sped up his thrusts, then followed her, shouting her name as he came.

By the time they made it out of her apartment, Charity still couldn't think straight. She was going to be late for work, and she needed some food after the workout she had been through in the last twenty-four hours.

"I think we should eat in tonight."

She glanced at him, as she stepped onto the elevator. "Is that so?"

He nodded and followed her onto the lift. "With everything up in the air, it will be easier to have a handle on things."

"It couldn't be that you just want to have hot monkey sex, could it?"

He punched the button for the first floor. He slipped his hand around her waist and pulled her closer. "That might be part of it. The other part is that I want to go over the case some more."

She shrugged. "No problem for me, but I don't have much in the house."

"I'll pick something up on the way home."

She nodded. When the doors slid open, she stepped out of the lift and found Drew standing there. "Hey, what are you doing here?"

He looked at the arm TJ had around her waist, then at her. "I thought we could ride together."

She looked at TJ. "You're behind this."

"Not really. Well, sort of. Both Delano and I think it best."

"There have yet to be any issues. In fact, it's speculation that anyone would target me."

"Hey, it's better safe than sorry. They see you with people, it will lower the chances."

She knew it was the smart thing to do. "Fine. But when y'all decide things like this, I don't want to be left out. It's not like I would disagree, but I don't like decisions being made for me. I'm an adult."

His mouth twitched. "Noted. And tell your boss."

He leaned closer and brushed his mouth over hers. "Behave today."

"See ya, later, Drew."

Drew said nothing as he watched him leave. "You're sleeping with him."

She glanced at the older woman who was now waiting for the elevator. Grabbing Drew's hand, she pulled him along to the door. "Not that it is any of your business, but yes, I am."

He said nothing for a long time.

"Your car or mine?" she asked.

"Yours. I walked over this morning, and I'm closer to work, if I need to get to the apartment."

They said nothing to each other as they walked to her car. He was one of her best friends, and had never passed judgment on the men she dated. *Ever.* He had always viewed them with amusement. His irritation with TJ was completely out of character. She knew jealousy was not part of it. He was no more interested in her than she was in him.

Once they were in her car, he finally spoke.

"It's not like you to do something like this."

"Leap without looking? I do it all the time."

She had her hand on the ignition ready to turn the car on, when he stopped her. "No. You like him. You like him a lot, and when you found out what was going on, it hurt you. You hid it from almost everyone, but I knew. I saw it. Now, he's practically living with you, and you're sleeping with him. I'm more than a little concerned."

Her heart softened. At the bottom of it all was that her friend was worried about her. She sighed.

"I know it's a different situation, and I might be doing something really stupid." He opened his mouth, but she stopped him. "But I don't care. I can't explain it, but he...well, he gets me. I know I date a lot—which loosely means I have a lot of ex-lovers. But the truth is, none of them really knew and accepted the geek side of me. Remember that one surfer I dated during the Eddie?"

"Jake. Just Jake," Drew said with the perfect imitation of Jake's surfer Cali accent.

"Yeah. I spent a week with him."

"He left sand all over your apartment."

That pulled a laugh from her. "Yeah, he did. I have no idea if he even had parents. And, when I explained the names of my cats, he seemed, put off by it. Like a girl like me isn't supposed to be into stuff like that."

"I get that. I do. But TJ lied to you."

She nodded. "And tell me if we were investigating the FBI, we wouldn't have done the same thing? I know Del likes to get pissed and talk about invading his house, but we all cut corners from time to time. I do thank God it was him and not another agent."

"Why?"

Constant Craving

"Other than the fact that I might just be addicted to his body—"

Drew made a gagging sound. "Ugh, gross."

"Another agent would not have looked under the surface. He did, and because of that, I'm not being set up. I know I would have gotten out of the mess, but he might have saved me months of aggravation."

"He hurt you."

"We're all human, Drew. Hurting each other is part of the game. It's what we do to make up for it that matters."

"Okay. But, if he does any kind of crap like he just pulled, I'm going to make him cry. It might not be physical, but Emma can help me really mess with him."

She smiled. "I would expect nothing less of you."

TJ actually made it into work, and started going through his emails. He was about half way through when Tsu popped his head in the door.

"Hey, how was the conference?" TJ asked.

"Not bad. Not that I learned anything, and it was cold and rainy."

"You were in Seattle."

He smiled. "How's that Foley case going?"

TJ shrugged. "Waiting on a warrant for some security video that could clear the subject."

Tsu shut the door behind him and walked into the office. He wasn't his usual laid back self. Something was really off.

"I've heard some rumors."

Fuck. Did he know TFH knew about the investigation?

TJ leaned back in his chair and tried to keep his voice smooth.

"About what?"

"Remington."

"What about him?"

"I talked to an old friend at the conference, who said he has a few marks against him because of this Foley incident. He said Remington didn't handle it well."

TJ shrugged. "Things went wrong. You know with undercover work sometimes things don't go right."

"Yes. But it seems that he's not been doing the rest of his work. He had a case taken away from him just last month."

That made TJ pause. "Why?"

"He's obsessed with Foley."

"Can you blame him?"

Tsu shook his head. "But, sometimes, you go too far off the edge of that cliff you have nothing to do but fall. I just wanted you to know all the facts."

"I appreciate it." And he did. Remington might have been his mentor, but Tsu was definitely a nicer boss. He understood that as an agent, you have to put up with a lot of bullshit. He always allowed for a level playing field for his agents.

"I gotta go handle my emails, which I'm sure are out of control."

"See ya, later, boss."

As the door closed behind Tsu, TJ thought about the situation. He was definitely not telling any of them about TFH knowing of the investigation. He'd wait on that. If Remington was going off the rails, he wanted to make sure he played this one close to his chest.

Constant Craving

It was then it struck him that he was picking Charity over the Bureau. Not really picking her, but choosing her side for the moment. Hell. He was picking her over his job. Six months ago, if someone had said he would be in this position, he would have called them a dirty liar. But now...things were different. Of course, that happened when you fell in love.

He blinked. He wasn't in love. That was just asinine. He barely knew the woman. People didn't fall in love with other people in the space of a week—no matter what stupid movies said. It just did not happen. It was hormones and some of the best sex of his life. It was all crowding out his ability to think. Once he sorted it all out, he would be on the straight and narrow again. Get back to his life.

The fact that getting back to his life without Charity left him feeling slightly queasy was a worry. Hell, right now, he wanted to call and check on her, but he didn't. Barely.

Shit. He was falling in love with her. In the middle of an investigation into activities the FBI had her linked to. He couldn't be in love. This wasn't the time, and it definitely wasn't the place. He always thought things through, and had planned on falling for a woman outside of law enforcement. One who would never know the dirty side of his life.

"What the hell am I thinking?"

You don't think when you're in love.

Well, shit. Why? Why now? Why this woman? He could walk away right now, maybe save himself. He wasn't completely in love with her. He was still falling. Maybe he could save himself the worry and the pain. The moment he thought that, he was already shaking his head. If he was going to be stuck with the woman, she was going to have to accept it. His mouth curved. And he had just the way to convince her.

Before he could get too stuck on how he would convince her, his email sounded. He'd gotten the warrant. The sooner they got the footage and looked it over, the sooner he could clear all of this up. And, the sooner he could figure out just what the hell to do about Charity.

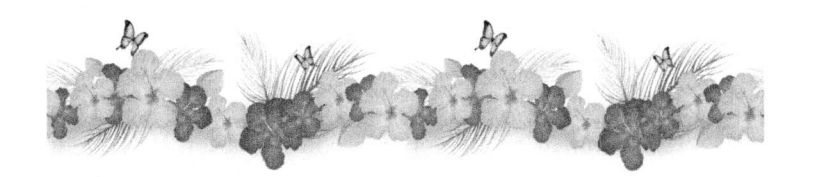

Chapter Twelve

Around eleven that morning, Charity rushed into the conference room about five minutes late, and was relieved to find everyone but Del there. He was still on the phone in his office. She was breathing heavy when she hurried over to the table.

"Whew, I thought I was late."

"You are late, lass," Graeme said with a smile. "But I'll no' tell him."

She snorted and took the open seat next to Drew. "Since he was staring at me when I came around the corner, there is a good chance Del knows."

"Yeah, I saw you," Del said as he walked into the room. "But since this was last minute, I'll cut you some slack."

"You are too gracious," she said.

The joke went unacknowledged, and she knew what the frown meant. Something had happened. Del was a good boss and never minded a little joking around. But, when he had that bulldog expression, something had just gone down. Considering the situation, she felt her stomach quiver.

"Is it the Foley case?"

He shook his head. "Nothing still on that. We need to talk about it, but we might have a case."

"Thank God. I thought I was going to be forced to sit through another terrorism briefing," Cat said.

Del shook his head. "You're still going to have to do that."

"Yeah, but I can pretend to listen while I think about another case."

"Hey," Marcus said. The former Capitol policeman was in charge of all the terrorism tasks for the TFH since he had the most experience with it.

She rolled her eyes. "I'm only there as backup. Everyone knows you're our expert on that. I take notes on the important things, but you know, they go on and on about crap that is a waste of time. Even Tamilya agrees."

"Tamilya is not always right," Marcus responded.

Cat let one eyebrow rise. "Have you said that to her? Either way, no one talks to me but you and Tamilya."

"That's because you challenged them to a shooting contest and won."

She smiled. "Aw, the fragile male egos I have to deal with."

"That's enough," Del said with no heat. "I got a call this morning from the governor. We have two dead males who used the same dating service. At first glance, it really doesn't scream connected case."

"On second glance?" Adam asked.

"I sent you the pics. The way they were killed, and the fact that all their money and valuables were gone, is a common thread. Throw in the dating service, and it is moving toward suspicious."

Constant Craving

Adam nodded and clicked a few buttons. Two young men, one Asian, the other white, appeared on the screen. They were both around the same age, perfect skin, hair, and teeth.

"The service they used was local, and very selective. Seems they only cater to the one percenter types. Or, local celebrities."

"Why did the governor call you?" Marcus asked.

"Mainly because of Charlie Xan there. He was the latest one, and his father is a huge donor."

"And there you go," Drew said. "I knew Charlie."

"Oh, Drew, I'm sorry," she said patting his hand.

He shook his head. "No worries. I knew him, didn't like him in particular. I mean, I definitely wouldn't want him to die, but he wasn't a nice guy."

"How well did you know him?" Del asked.

"Not very. We went to high school together. He was kind of a jerk."

"In what way?"

"His family was one of the richest in school—and that is saying a lot." Drew had gone to Punahou. It was the most expensive school on the island, and boasted President Obama as one of its alumni. "He also did not have a problem letting everyone know it. Drove the best car, dated the most popular girls, and loved to pick on the nerds. He never got in trouble for it either. Really spoiled."

Del nodded. "That's what I'm hearing. He was in the middle of a divorce and using a dating service before his wife filed."

"What a bastard," Elle said.

"And his former wife is being investigated. Or will be.

Adam, I want you to look at that. As well as a few of the women he was dating at the time."

Adam nodded. "So, you're basically saying that a bunch of women wanted him dead?"

"Yeah."

"What about the other victim?" Charity asked.

"Patrick Denney. He's new to the islands, meaning that he's only been here ten years."

That brought a smile from her. She knew that locals always considered anyone from the mainland new to the islands. It took years to gain the respected title as *Kamaʻāina*.

"And their only connection is the service, and the manner they were killed. So, what I need is some digging, mainly from you, Charity. I would have Emma do it, but she's got an appointment this morning and a video conference with someone in Tokyo later. Plus, I don't want to pull her in unless it turns into a case. I'm also worried this may take a few months, and she will be preoccupied in a few weeks with the baby. I want you to take the lead on that area and just ask her for advice. That way you will be familiar with the situation. The rest of you, I wanted you aware of the situation. And we need to talk about our federal situation."

Everyone looked at her. "Hey, don't blame me."

"Do you know if the warrant came through yet?" Adam asked.

"TJ said it would be this morning, probably."

"Good, let us know as soon as you do. Anything else?" Del asked.

She shook her head.

"Good, that's it."

Constant Craving

Everyone got up to leave and she asked Del, "Did you send me everything you have?"

"Yep, should be in your inbox by now."

"I'm off to work, while the rest of you laze about."

She hurried out, her mind on the task at hand. She always fared better when she had a project, and this one sounded promising.

"Who's holding the bet on this one?" Marcus asked as soon as both Charity and Del were outside of earshot.

"Emma was holding the money on it I think."

Drew said nothing. He had inside knowledge, but he was worried about his friend. Getting involved with a man like Callahan wasn't always good, especially for someone with a soft heart like Charity.

"Drew?"

"What?"

"I asked if you had spoken to Emma today?"

He shook his head. "I knew she had an appointment."

Del walked into the office and they all turned to him. "What?"

"Nothing. Talking about lunch," Cat said.

He didn't look like he believed them, but he just waved and walked out the door.

Once Del was out of earshot again, they started talking.

"I'll call her later," Graeme said. "There is something definitely up with our Georgia Peach."

Drew continued his silence. Charity had been the one person who had helped him through his anger. Others had tried, but they had handled him with kid gloves. Charity had been a different story. She hadn't asked him to move in with her. She had rented a truck and shown up at his parents' house. Two hours later, he was unpacking his things in her guest room. Charity wouldn't take no for an answer.

As he and Elle headed downstairs to the morgue, she smiled at him. "I can tell you, I'm so happy to have you back."

He gave her a smile, but his mind was on Charity. As they stepped off the elevator, Elle headed to her office. "Come on, we need to chat."

He nodded and followed. Elle sat behind her desk, and he sat in one of the two chairs she had for guests.

"Spit it out, Drew. Are you not happy about being back?"

He finally focused on his supervisor. She was frowning at him and he realized, she was concerned. "No. I mean; I *am* happy about being back."

"Then what has you looking so upset?"

He sighed. "Charity."

"I'm worried about her too."

He didn't want to reveal too much. Charity was one of his best friends, and he respected her privacy, but his concern overrode some of that.

"She's not acting like she normally does with a guy," Drew said. "She doesn't get this involved."

"You're not jealous?"

He snorted. "Not likely. You know we see each other as brother and sister."

"Then what is it?"

"It's this Callahan. He's got her tangled up in something that could hurt her. And I don't trust him."

"Those are good instincts, as he lied to all of us."

Drew nodded. "And that is a big no no for Charity. Lying has always been a deal breaker. You know how she is. She has no problem dating a construction worker one night and then going out with a professor the next. She loves all kinds of men, but she has one thing she will not allow. Lying. But this guy breaks that deal, and she lets it go. I think she isn't thinking straight, and she could end up hurt."

Elle's expression softened. "You're such a sweet man, Drew, but both of us know that without risk, there is no reward."

"That sounds like bullshit."

Elle laughed. "Yeah, well, I have to agree, but it's also true. Charity is interested in the man. I can't blame her."

"Can I tell Graeme that?"

"Stop being cheeky. This *is* your first week back."

His humor faded as he thought about his friend. "Her involvement with him is different. Like it is a new level of something."

"I saw that from the beginning and worried about it."

"And?"

Elle didn't speak at first. He knew that meant she wanted to choose every word very carefully. "Charity has always been very open about her feelings. I envied her ability to accept the here and now, and not look beyond that. Living in the moment must be wonderful. But with Agent Callahan, I sense she feels something more for him."

"Again, that's what worries me."

"And in the end, as friends, all we can do is allow her to do what she feels she needs to do."

"What do we do when it goes to shit?"

"*If* it does, the only thing you can do is be there for her."

He shook his head. "I hate it, but I guess there is nothing for it."

She patted his hand. "You are a very sweet man, because most people wouldn't worry."

"I have been telling you for over a year now that I am the sweetest man you know. So, are you going to leave that idiot for me?"

She laughed. "I have a feeling you might have a fight on your hands."

"And that is one thing I am glad to hear."

Charity arrived home just after six that evening, and did not find Luke and Jess waiting for her. Even when Drew lived with her, they had always greeted her at the door. She shut the door behind her, then slipped off her shoes. The smell of tomatoes, basil, and garlic hit her. She turned the corner and found TJ in her kitchen. Her cats, the damned traitors, were sitting on the floor right beside him, watching his every move.

He had rolled his work shirt up and had a towel draped over his shoulder.

"Well, this is a pretty sight."

He turned to her with a smile. "Hey. How was work?"

"Okay. We might have a new case, so I got caught up in some research."

He turned down the heat and then threw a little salt into the pan. "Anything you can tell me?"

"A couple of guys with a dating service turned up dead after dates."

"Oh?"

She shrugged. "There were six months between each of the hits, but the last one was the son of one of the Governor's biggest contributors. You know the dog and pony show that goes with that." She stepped up next to him. "Whatcha making?"

"I thought some pasta would be nice tonight." He grabbed a spoon and dipped it in the sauce. After blowing on it, he offered it to her.

"I thought you were just going to pick something up."

He shook his head. "I haven't been able to cook in about a month, thanks to the rehab on the kitchen. Try it. I promise it's good."

She allowed him to slip the spoon into her mouth. Tomatoes, garlic, basil...with just a hint of heat. "Oh, God, that's not good. That's a religious experience."

"Mama's recipe."

"Then, thank your mother for that."

He smiled and leaned down to brush his mouth against hers. "Hey, there."

She smiled. "Hey, there yourself."

"Dinner should be ready in about fifteen minutes," he said, as he dumped a package of rigatoni into some boiling water.

"Sounds good," she said. "Do you need any help?"

"Not really."

"Great, then I will go change into something more comfortable." She rose up on her toes and kissed his cheek. "Be right back."

When she left, her cats stayed. Of course they did. She didn't blame them. Hot man, good food...who could resist that?

She slipped out of her shirt and skirt, and grabbed a Pokémon t-shirt. She hesitated. Most people would say it was out of character for her. She loved to dress up, wear the pretty dresses and skirts, four-inch heels and keep her toes painted. The truth was, she had so many different styles. One day she would dress for success, the next day she was wearing board shorts and a bikini top. Slipping the shirt on, she smiled. With TJ, she felt completely comfortable with all her different moods.

She grabbed a pair of the aforementioned shorts, stepped into them, then joined him back in the kitchen.

"How about we eat on the lanai?" she asked.

"That sounds great," he said.

They worked easily in the kitchen together, and it was nice to have someone to share this part of the day with. Drew had been here, but he wasn't a cook. He had spent most of his life in a kitchen, and he hated it. In fact, it pained his mother that Drew preferred a Big Mac to homemade food. So, while he was there, cooking together had not been an option. Having someone there in the kitchen with her was nice.

When they had everything ready, they took their meals, along with a nice chianti, out to her lanai.

"So, I got the warrant today. We should get that footage and clear you."

She nodded as relief moved through her. "Great. That would be really great."

"It worries me though."

"Why?"

"Once we clear you, you might become a target."

She shook her head. "Highly unlikely."

She almost crossed her fingers when she said it, but she

did believe it. There was no reason to come after her. She had been a ruse, someone to confuse the issue.

"Why do you say that?"

"While I am still in the balance like I am now, I could be a target. But, once I am clear, there is nothing that can be done."

"And?"

She knew he was a smart man, had to be clever to get to where he was. So the fact that he wasn't seeing the situation for what it was worried her.

"Right now, they could use me. They could hurt me or kill me, and that would leave them to do whatever they are planning and pin it on me. Foley, or his accomplice, could easily tie me to it. If you had not been put on the job, things might not have moved along the way they did. A lesser agent would have pinned it on me, even. You, though, think outside of the box."

There was a faint color to his cheeks and she laughed.

"As I live and breathe, Thor Jackson is blushing."

"I am not. And don't use that name."

"Why not? It's your name."

He shook his head, apparently not ready to argue with her. "You did bring up a good point. What if this is just a red herring?"

She blinked. "What?"

"Well, my boss went to a conference this weekend."

"Remington?"

"No, Tsu, my supervisor here. Remington hasn't been my supervisor for a year."

"Do you want to tell me what happened?"

He shrugged as he set his fork down. "It was an undercover op. I didn't make contact with Rebecca, but I was shadowing her, like I said."

"Rebecca. She's the woman who was killed?"

He nodded. "Yeah. She had been working with Foley. Remington had found her, pretty easily. Worked at the State Department, and had been giving Foley secrets for months."

"Was he paying her?"

"Not that we can tell. They had a few weekends together, but the last six months of her life, she had only been contacted by email and text from him."

"Oh, then she did it for love?"

"That's what it read like. No matter what we did, we couldn't trace him. When we would get a lead, it would evaporate. Then, in the end, when he had gotten everything he wanted—or we got too close—he killed her. I got there just as the bastard was fleeing."

"And got shot?" He nodded. "That's the scar I saw on your back?"

He nodded. "It wasn't that bad, especially since we already had emergency services on the way. Rebecca was gone by the time they got there, though."

She shook her head. "I have heard something like that with every case connected to Foley. Three years ago, didn't he kill some do-gooder who thought he was helping expose corrupt government officials?"

TJ nodded. "And I do understand being obsessed. I had been for a while, but when I realized how unhealthy it was, I stepped away."

"And came to Hawaii," she said with a smile.

He returned it. "Anyway, Tsu said that there was talk that Remington is losing his clout."

Constant Craving

She frowned. "How so?"

"He's been missing meetings on other cases. He even had one taken away from him last week. Ever since our failure with Foley, he has been falling apart. Not just on the job, but also at home apparently. Having rumors spread about you in the agency is never good. The rumor is that he is obsessed with Foley."

"Yeah? It would make sense though. You were injured and he lost a civilian."

"All of us were at fault for that."

She cocked her head to the side and studied him. She thought about what Tamilya said. Captain America. Yeah, he would try and take on some of the blame, but she couldn't let him. "He was the boss. Sucks, but it is true. He should have had a better handle on it."

TJ didn't rise to defend his old boss.

"I wouldn't have agreed with you just a few weeks ago, but I did some digging on him. He's been divorced, and is practically living out of his office. I'm starting to question his opinion on Foley, and on whatever led him to you."

She thought about that. "I would reserve judgment. Obsession doesn't always mean someone is wrong. It just means the rest of their life is crap."

He smiled. "I can agree with that. So, tell me about this case of yours." The talk turned to other things, her case, Drew's behavior, and the bets that were being thrown around.

The man the FBI knew as Foley knew something was wrong. Things didn't seem to be running as smoothly as before. He was sure someone had been listening in on his phone calls, which meant that his house and car were probably bugged. Now, repeated calls to his handler had gone unanswered. He couldn't recall a time when he could not get hold of him.

He shoved a hand through his thinning hair and tried his best to swallow. His mouth was dry. He had left his office in downtown DC and headed out for the suburbs of Fairfax. The mall. It was always a safe bet. A person could disappear there. The sun was just starting to set as he locked his car and walked to the entrance.

Something cold slithered down his spine, even as he felt another bead of sweat on his temple. He wiped it away and started to walk faster. It had been a mistake. At first, the whole thing seemed so easy. Pose as me, pretend to be the man in charge of everything. It had been a thrill at first. He couldn't deny that. A government employee who worked in accounting didn't have a lot of excitement. This provided it. Then, it had gotten dangerous. Really dangerous. Soon, he had blood on his hands, and he had no way out.

He breathed a sigh of relief when he entered the air-conditioned facility and started to walk among the shoppers. Maybe here he could get lost and maybe, just maybe, he could figure a way out.

Chapter Thirteen

Charity insisted on cleaning up since TJ had cooked. He had no problem with that. It was a rule in the Callahan household too. His mother refused to clean up after a meal when she had four healthy men in her household eating.

After storing the leftovers in the fridge, Charity started on the dishes. He sat on the breakfast bar and watched. It wasn't that he was a man who was into watching a woman do domestic duties. It had more to do with Charity. TJ just liked watching the way she moved. There was something almost lyrical to the way her hips would sway as she walked. Now, though, as he watched, steam rose up from the water and had him thinking of other things. When she glanced up at him, she smiled.

"I have to give it to you. That was about the best red sauce I have had—and that is saying a lot. I dated a chef for a while, who specialized in Italian dishes."

"I guess I can't get my ego hurt that you mentioned an ex when you say my sauce was better than his."

She chuckled. "It was. I would never tell him that, because, he was a chef and prone to outbursts. But, his red sauce was a little bland for my liking."

"Are we still talking about his sauce?"

She rolled her eyes, but she was still smiling. "Don't be cheeky as Elle would say."

"Noted."

"But, back to the sauce. I like that little bite it had to it."

"Crushed red pepper. Just a couple dashes. Mom always liked to add a little. She says being a Texan, she was eating chili before she was two years old."

She nodded as she rinsed off the stock pot he had boiled the pasta in. She set it in the drying rack and started on the skillet. "Now, I'll have to cook something to pay you back. Do you like Mahi?"

"I like just about any kind of fish," he said, rising and joining her at the counter. He grabbed a clean towel and started to dry the pot.

"Great. I'll get some tomorrow. It's that or I can make some fried shrimp."

"Beer battered?" he asked.

She nodded. "Along with some cornbread."

He grabbed her and pulled her to him. "Don't mess with me, woman."

She smiled, and it made his heart do a little jig. "I can promise you, I make some damned good cornbread. I can do super sweet or cheese and jalapeño."

"Let's go with sweet," he said. She moved as if to step away, but he held on and pulled her even closer. "Hey."

"What?"

Constant Craving

For a moment, his brain stopped working. Just went completely blank.

"TJ?"

He shrugged. "I kind of missed you today."

What made him say that? It was true, but he rarely revealed so much to a woman this early in the relationship. Strike that. He rarely shared this much at all. It was one of the things his exes had complained about. It was why he had so many exes. What was it about her that made him reveal things he usually kept hidden?

Then, a second later, her expression softened. There was that jig again. He couldn't remember *ever* feeling this way about a woman, especially one he did not know that well. He knew the facts about her, her background, her family history, but he wasn't sure he knew her that well.

But you do.

Internally, he chastised his inner voice. He did not need stupid actions during this. He knew she was good and decent, and that was one of the reasons he was sure she was innocent. This fast, he was tangled up with her. And in years past, he might have objected...or maybe he hadn't recognized it. But with this woman, she was getting to him. Every little thing she did got to him. And now he was quoting damned *Police* songs in his head.

He pushed those thoughts aside and bent his head.

He meant the kiss to be sweet...just a tempting treat of what was to come. But it only took a second for it to turn carnal. She moaned, the sound of it slipped over him. Taking her face in his hands, he deepened the kiss, stealing inside for a taste. The heat of the sauce, the taste of wine, and then the essence of Charity danced over his taste buds. It made him think of other tastes, needs...desires.

He backed her up against the opposite counter without breaking the kiss. Pulling away, he lifted her up by the waist and set her on the counter. He eased her shorts down her legs, then slipped his fingers beneath the waistband of her panties. As he pulled them down her legs, his fingers shivered. TJ was a man who liked to take his time, liked to savor women, but with Charity, he seemed to have no control; wanting her now, right here.

He tossed the panties behind him, not caring where they landed. Dropping to his knees, he placed a hand on the inside of each thigh. He pressed against them, spreading her out. She was already wet. Leaning closer, he pressed his mouth to her. That unique taste, the need she had for him, burst through him as he dipped his tongue inside of her sex. Over and over, he thrust his tongue into her. He added a finger, as he used his mouth to tease her clit. Within seconds, she was coming apart, her hands molded to the back of his head, as she chanted his name over and over.

When her shivers had subsided, he picked her up, and strode to her bedroom.

"TJ," she said, her voice just above a whisper. He turned to look at her and she kissed him.

He tripped over his feet. He righted himself and made it into the bedroom—barely. Setting her down on her feet, he started to undress her. She batted his hands away and started to do it herself.

"Sit down, Thor."

Her mouth curved into the evilest of smiles, as she took a step back. He hated to relinquish control, anywhere, but particularly in the bedroom. He liked to be the one in charge. But the gleam in her eyes told him that it would probably benefit him to give in this once.

He surrendered and did as she ordered.

With extreme care, she peeled off her shirt. His fingers itched to touch, but instead, he fisted his hands in the comforter. She continued her lazy pace, skimming her hands over her own flesh. How he was sitting there without passing out, he did not know. There was definitely no blood left in his brain. She slipped her bra off, letting it fall to the floor. Then, with that same secretive smile, she slid her hands back down her body.

The woman was killing him inch by inch. Again, she skimmed her hands over her own flesh, caressing her soft skin; first on her belly, then up to her breasts. His cock ached. He was damned close to losing all control. Need spiraled higher than ever before, as he tried to keep himself in check. He wanted to touch, to taste. She pinched each of her nipples, then her hands roamed down to in between her legs. He knew she would be wet, ready for his hands, his mouth, his cock. His licked his lips and she chuckled. TJ glanced up and saw it. The power of the woman, the need to control the situation, to have him on her terms. It was fucking intoxicating.

Stepping between his legs, she started to unbutton his shirt. He paid no attention to her hands because her breasts were eye level. Ignoring them was just not in him. He leaned forward and licked first one, then the other. She shuddered, causing them to sway. TJ could no longer resist. He took one hardened tip into his mouth as he teased the other.

She moaned as she yanked off his shirt. When her hands

were free, she slipped her fingers through his hair and urged him closer. Then, she pulled away.

"We have *got* to get you naked," she said, with a laugh. Again, his heart felt lighter at the sound. She accomplished her task in record time, and was kneeling between his legs before he could even think straight.

"I want to take my time tonight. I didn't get to play with your body nearly enough last night."

She wrapped her hand around his cock and stroked him before bending her head. He watched her, unable to take a breath. Charity looked up at him with those golden eyes, as she took him into her mouth. Right then and there, he almost lost it and came. She hummed and added her hand as she continued to tease him. God, the woman was going to be the death of him. He was half out of his mind, ready to lose it, when she pulled away and urged him back on the bed. She joined him with a condom, rolling it down on his cock, then straddling his hips.

Rising up, she grabbed hold of his shaft and sunk down on it. She was slow about it, leaning her head back and moaning as she did it.

It was the most erotic thing he might have ever seen in his life.

Then, she started to ride him. She took him deep again and again, as he grabbed hold of her hips. She batted his hands away, leaning down, but continuing to gyrate her hips.

His orgasm approached, and he wasn't quite sure he could hold back any longer. She rose up again, pulling him with her, and holding him tight. She started to come again, and he gave into his own release. As he let loose a shout, she bent her head and kissed him. In it he felt her need for him, for this connection. They fell back on the bed together, still joined.

The next day, TJ stepped into his office just as his cell started to ring. He knew it was Remington, and he wasn't in the mood. But, there was one thing you couldn't do at the FBI, avoid a cell phone call. Bastards would figure out just what you were doing, he thought with a smile.

"Callahan," he said.

"Hey, we've been going over that footage and have yet to find Edwards. Right now, it looks like the trip to LA might have been a ruse, just as I expected."

The bottom fell out of TJ's stomach. "Is that a fact?"

"Yeah. I'm not ready to pull her in, not yet. But, I want to make sure that you were aware of the situation."

"Of course."

"Did you have anything to report?"

"No. Everything else seems on the up and up."

"I was looking at the financial reports on her. She seems to have a lot of cash."

"Family money. She was left a trust from her grandfather on her father's side. She barely touched it for college, since she had scholarships. From what I can tell, she's been investing it for a few years and it has done well."

"Hmm, still it could be a cover."

Dammit, when Remington had his teeth in something like this, he rarely let go. It was one of the things that had helped him move up in the FBI, but it had also kept him back in certain cases. The single-mindedness was seen as a hindrance to being a good supervisor.

"Anything else?"

"No, not now. Just keep on working the job. When we need to pull her in, I'll give you a call."

He clicked off his phone as his mind started to work over the problem. Something was off. TJ knew she had gone to LA. Knew it to be a fact down to his bones. Even without that, she had a picture of her and her parents at Disneyland. There wasn't a doubt in his mind that Charity was innocent. It definitely smelled like a setup, but if he mentioned that to Remington at this point, his former boss would say he was missing the bigger picture.

He checked his schedule and realized he had a staff meeting at ten, but after that, he was heading back into Honolulu. He needed to talk to the TFH folks and see if they could get their hands on the footage. For a long moment, he sat there and stared at his computer screen. When did he become someone willing to break ranks and break the law? He had always followed orders—as long as they were lawful. Now, he was playing outside the lines...and for what reason?

Charity.

The answer was simple to him. In less than two weeks, she had become so damned important to him. It was stupid...insane even. It could also be a career ending action. He had worked long and hard to get to where he was at the FBI. Putting it all on the line for a woman who might be helping a man steal millions of secrets to sell on the dark net didn't sound like TJ Callahan, he thought. But, then, he knew Charity. In the short time they'd been acquainted, he had come to know the woman pretty well. He knew she could not do this. It just wasn't in her makeup. Oh, sure, she would hack things for fun, or even to find out info for a case, but she would never sell secrets. And, she wasn't involved with a man other than TJ.

He decided to get his work done and get ready for the meeting so that when it was done, he could head out to see her and the team. They would definitely be able to figure out what was going on.

TJ was pacing back and forth in Charity's small office. He had arrived ten minutes earlier in an agitated state. He was pissed and rambling on about the case. Some of it she could figure out, but a lot of it was just irritated mumbling. Her father did something similar and, as she had learned a lot from her mother, she did just as her mother did. She stayed out of his way and waited. He was working through some things in his head, and there was no soothing his temper. Not right now.

"It makes no sense," she said. Before he could say anything else, Emma and Del walked into her office. As soon as TJ had told her about the news this morning, she had called them in. Del, because he was the boss, and Emma, because she was the smartest person Charity knew.

"Hey, so what's up?" Emma asked.

"The footage from LAX was missing any sign of Charity."

"Why didn't you get footage from Honolulu?"

He sighed. "We've had cases of people going through security at the home base, then just turning around and leaving. Having her here means less if she never arrived at LAX."

"I went to LA," she said.

He looked at her, his eyes narrowed as he studied her. "Of course you went. The problem is that the LAX footage is screwed up in some way."

"What I don't get is that if she was in LA, she could have still hacked into the servers here, right?" Del asked. "And didn't we prove that someone sent an attachment to her computer, and that's the way the hacker got in?"

"Yeah, but there must be something else that makes them think she was here," Emma said, looking at TJ.

He held up his hands. "Hey, they didn't tell me."

"But it is a good point," Charity murmured. "Did they have some kind of information they didn't give you?"

TJ shrugged, and he looked even more irritated. "And I would say it was more of a *him* than a *they*. I'm not sure if the FBI is interested in you or if it's Remington."

"Why does he seem to have a hard-on for Charity?" Del asked.

"That is a very good question," Emma said. "Have you met this Remington before?"

Charity shook her head. "I went to a few lectures when I was in DC where he was on a panel, but I have never met him personally. I'm pretty sure he didn't know me.

"He does."

"Why do you say that?" she asked TJ.

"He mentioned that the FBI tried to recruit you and they he had attended some of *your* lectures."

"Yeah, the FBI did. The CIA offered a better deal."

"That doesn't mean he really knows who she is," Emma pointed out. "He just had a good file on her."

TJ nodded. "True."

"We need to find out why it is important to tie her to Honolulu," Emma said.

"Yeah. Remington must know something he isn't telling me."

"What I don't get is why they zeroed in on Charity in the first place?" Emma said.

"What do you mean?" Charity asked.

"I'm the better hacker. Well known, in fact—at least in certain circles. I'm pretty sure the FBI has a fairly thick file. So, why not pick me?"

"You are only considered a contractor here," Del said.

"True."

Then she got what Emma was getting at. "Yeah, it would make more sense to check you out. You aren't bound by any oaths or, hell, you don't really need the work."

"But you're married to me."

Emma gave her husband a pitying glance. "If I was dirty, you would never know it."

He smiled. "I would know."

"Still, there is a big reason they didn't use Emma. She has ties on the island. A half-brother and now Del," Charity pointed out. "All I have is a job."

"But you bought an apartment," Emma pointed out.

"Easily sold on today's market, or could be profitable as a rental. I have no family ties here. Plus, add in buying a massive apartment at one of the premiere complexes in Honolulu, that would raise red flags. Emma has money, well documented, but I don't talk much about my family business. I also used most of it to pay for the apartment so I could live without a mortgage."

"But why Hawaii?" TJ asked. "This just doesn't make sense."

"Maybe the person lives here. The one working for Foley. That would give him time to research me."

TJ nodded. "That's been brought up before, but still, something is bothering me about it. It's just odd."

"The first thing to do is get our hands on the footage. Where did you stay? Any hotels?" Emma asked.

Charity shook her head. "Dad rented a house for the week. But...there might be something at Disneyland. We spent the entire day there."

Emma nodded. "That might be harder to screw with. Disney has better security than LAX."

Del looked at his wife. "And how would you know that?"

"Everyone knows that," she said. More than likely, Emma thought everyone did know that. Charity knew there was a good chance her friend had breached it more than once.

"I have to give the governor a call about that other case," Del said.

"I'll let you know what I find," Emma said as he dragged her out of Charity's office.

"I understand why she isn't doing it here, but where is she going?"

"Probably to her brother's. He's got a massive system in his house in Kailua. It is almost impossible for people to trace." She waited for him to comment, but he didn't. "No recriminations for breaking the law?"

Constant Craving

He raised his gaze to hers. The intensity of it stole her breath. "No. This is life or death, and I can't let you take the fall for a Foley stooge."

"Someday I am going to need to give Remington a big fat kiss."

His eyebrows shot up. "Yeah? Why?"

"The fact that he called you in on this case probably saved me a lot of grief and money. I don't think someone else would have looked beyond the reports on me."

His expression softened and he rose from the chair. He walked around the desk, and turned her to face him. Setting his hands on the arms of her chair, he leaned down and brushed his mouth against hers. The simple gesture should have just been that. Simple. Instead, her heart started to race and her blood heated. He pulled back and rested his forehead against hers. "I wanted to take you to lunch, but I have to get back to work."

"That would have been nice, but I understand."

He straightened as he studied her face.

"What?"

He shrugged.

"Thor Jackson, you better tell me."

"You use that name again and I will have you arrested and taken to a secret CIA site."

She laughed. "Try it. Remember, I'm former CIA. I can definitely mess with your life."

TJ smiled. "So, this is a battle of the government agencies?"

"Go. I have work to do."

"See you tonight."

And then he was gone. Charity sat there for a long time, waiting for the panic. From the time she was allowed to start dating, she had avoided long relationships. She didn't like the idea of being tied down. First, school was too important to her. Then, her career. It wasn't as if she'd suffered from lack of male attention. She'd had her share of dates. She had even had men she called her boyfriend from time to time—until they asked for more than just right now.

But with TJ, it was something else. She couldn't put her finger on it, not really. She just felt comfortable with him. She liked how they were together, and he never had an issue with her intelligence. Many men say they don't have a problem, but it was usually a lie. When challenged, they would always falter. She had found that out when she worked for the CIA. Men were okay with her being smart until they got involved. Then, they expected her to take a backseat to them...even at work.

TJ was different. When he found out information, he came to her with it. They talked about it and, while he might not always agree with her, he listened to her. He respected her.

Why was that more intriguing than the billionaire who had flown her to Paris for a weekend? Hell, she'd had a pro football player who had wanted them to move in together, but he didn't make her feel the way TJ did. It took one look, one brush of his mouth against hers, and she was ready to jump his bones.

She closed her eyes and drew in a deep breath. Releasing it slowly, she opened her eyes. She was falling for him. Hard. He was so good, so full of the right kind of qualities, but there was no doubt in her mind that he would fight to the end for her. He was going to do everything in his power to make sure she was safe.

What would happen when it was all over? She had no idea, but she was pretty sure this time, it wouldn't be that easy to walk away.

Chapter Fourteen

By Friday, TJ was ready to punch a hole in the wall. They were no closer to finding anything out about the case. Remington hadn't called TJ, at least that was one good thing. A few texts and an email, but that was all. It was odd, and he wondered how much of the investigation was on the up and up. Was Remington trying to distance himself, or was he just being cautious?

"You need to quit grinding your teeth," Charity said as she studied him from across the desk.

He forced himself away from his dark thoughts to really look at her. "What?"

She laughed. "You don't realize you do it, do you?"

He shook his head. "That shows you how frustrated I am. We should be somewhere by now."

She stood up and walked over to him. Then, without another word, she plopped down in his lap. "Now, why is it that you are more worried about the case than I am?"

"You *are* the case."

She blinked. "What?"

He sighed as he rested his hand against the outside of her thigh. She smelled good, but she always did. Even after a hard bout of sex, there was that sweet womanly smell to her.

"I need to do this. Thanks to my involvement, you're a target."

"Oh." She was quiet for a long stretch. "First, it wasn't your involvement. It is the bastard who is helping Foley. Secondly, we have no evidence that Foley or his surrogate has targeted me after the fact. Maybe the whole idea was that I was a red herring so you would avoid the more likely suspect."

He frowned. It wasn't something they had not discussed before. Truth was, they had discussed the damned thing to death. He wanted this over. He wanted to get on with his life. He wanted to have more with Charity than this case.

It was sad to admit, but in the two weeks they had known each other, he had thought more about the future than any of his previous relationships. He had lived with a girlfriend in college, and he had never contemplated what would come next. Maybe it was his age, but he was sure most of it was the woman. She hadn't been Charity.

Before he could tell her what he had been thinking, Emma came tearing into the office. Well, as fast as an 8-month pregnant woman could move.

Charity tried to stand up, but he held onto her tightly. He wasn't embarrassed by their relationship, and she would have to get used to it.

"Hey, we have something. I have something."

Del smiled indulgently, as he stood behind her. "She's been talking like that since she arrived a few minutes ago."

Emma pulled out several pieces of paper from her

messenger bag and handed them to Charity. Charity and he looked at the screenshots that Emma had ran off. The stamped time was at the bottom of the picture. And there, dressed in a white and red polka dot dress, was Charity. A few days later, she was seen leaving, wearing a pair of Mickey ears. He had seen them in her room.

"These prove it," Charity said.

"I'm at a loss as to why they haven't found it at the FBI," TJ said.

"I have a theory on that," Emma said.

He looked up and found her smile had been replaced by a solemn expression. Before she said it, he knew what she was going to say.

"You might have a mole in the FBI."

"Damn."

"You're not disagreeing?" Del asked.

TJ shook his head. "I mentioned it before and I have assumed all along Foley might have someone working with him in the FBI. He always seems to be one step ahead of us."

"With that in mind, I'm going to ask you to keep this from your supervisors at the FBI, unless we need it."

He looked at Charity, then looked at Del. "Agree."

"Wait, what did that mean?" Charity asked.

"Nothing."

She frowned, and Emma apparently decided to take control of the conversation.

"What he means is that if the FBI comes back and tries to bring you in to question, we keep this in our back pocket."

"You don't think that will happen, do you?"

TJ shrugged. "I'm worried that nothing has happened yet to you."

"Well, thanks a lot."

"No. You were singled out, or this office was, for a reason. We have yet to realize the reason."

"It's probable that this was all a diversion. They picked us because we are out on our own and not tied directly to HPD," Emma said. "There is always a chance they are done with us."

"But I pulled Charity into this."

"No, you didn't," Charity said. "Whoever this asshole is pulled me into it. Not you."

"So, agreed that we don't reveal what we know. We don't know who is listening to what," Del said.

TJ nodded. "I could ask and find out who is going over the footage."

"We'll wait," Del said.

"I might be able to find out without us alerting anyone," Emma said.

"You have contacts at the FBI?" he asked.

"Yeah. Contacts with contacts." She rubbed a hand over her stomach. "I'm hungry."

Then she turned to leave without another word.

"She's kind of scary," TJ said.

"Yeah. One of the things I love best about her. We'll call if we hear anything."

"I guess we can go home," Charity said after they were alone.

"Yeah. I was thinking."

"About what?" she asked.

"How about we go up to Giovanni's and get some shrimp?"

She glanced at the clock. It was just before four. "We would be cutting it close."

"We can go to the one in Kahuku. They're open until six-thirty."

"Sounds fantastic."

They were on their way out of the building when they ran into Drew. TJ would rather avoid the man. He did not hide his disgust of TJ. But, TJ knew that if he was going to be in Charity's life, he was going to have to accept Drew. That also meant that TJ needed to get Drew to accept him.

"Hey, there, Drew. What do you have planned tonight?" Charity asked him.

"Mom's trying to get me to come over to the house. They have a church thing..."

"Oh, no," Charity said. "A set up. See, this is why I don't live in Atlanta."

"Why don't you come with us?" TJ asked. They both looked at him as if he'd lost his mind.

"We're going to Giovanni's for dinner."

Drew looked back and forth between them, then said, "Sure. I need to change."

"So do I. Do you need a ride?"

"Naw. I walked because it's just so damned close. I don't need my car here."

"We'll pick you up, if that is okay," TJ said.

Drew nodded and headed off in the direction of his apartment.

"What was that about?"

He shrugged. "I think we got off to a bad start, plus, I understand the whole parents trying to fix you up with someone."

"Is that a fact?"

He nodded. "Mom tried to fix me up with Dad's best friend's daughter. It was a disaster from start to finish."

"Is that a fact?"

"Yeah," he said thinking back. "She was kind of girly."

Charity stopped and stared at him. "I'm girly."

He chuckled when he thought about the Minnie Mouse-inspired dress she wore to LA. "Yeah, but you know how to shoot and fish. I like balance."

Her frown smoothed out. "That's true."

"Don't smile at me like that, woman. We have Drew expecting to be picked up. You look at me like that, and we won't get out of the apartment."

She laughed and hurried to her car. "Then we better get going so we can get back."

Drew had just started walking down the sidewalk when he heard his name called. Without looking, he knew who it was, and a small part of him, a very small part of him, almost kept walking. The childish urge to pretend he had not heard Cat's voice nearly won out.

Unfortunately, his mother had raised him better. Drew stopped and then pulled in a deep breath before he turned to face her. The impact of Cat Kalakau never seemed to fade. She always took his breath away.

She jogged toward him, a smile on her lips. Her long black hair was secured in a massive braid that bounced against her back with her movements. The TFH t-shirt was tucked into jeans, and she wore her trademark black boots. Her eyes were hidden behind mirrored sunglasses.

"Hey, I was trying to catch you before you headed out. What are you up to this weekend?"

She spoke casually, as if they had not had a romantic night of dancing...and a bit more...before she bolted the next day. Sure, he had been shot and almost died, but when she failed to appear at the hospital—then not once visited him while he was recuperating—she told him exactly how she felt about their relationship.

"I'm going out tonight."

Sure, it was with Charity and TJ, but she didn't need to know that. She lost that privilege when she hadn't returned his calls.

She slipped off her sunglasses. "Oh, because I was thinking about heading out to Dave's Ice Cream later and getting a few scoops."

It was his favorite place on the island to get ice cream, and they had often gone after work. She knew that, and at one time, he would have jumped at the chance. But now, he couldn't.

He shrugged. "Sorry. I've got plans for the weekend."

"Oh. Family?"

He shook his head and said nothing. She had no right to know that he really wasn't doing anything much at all. She was no longer part of his life like that. Part of him hurt to know that, but the bigger part of him knew he needed to keep away from her, away from the feelings she brought out in him.

"Oh. Okay."

Then she said nothing.

"Is there something else, Cat?"

For the first time since he had known Cat, she fidgeted. She looked down the street, then she played with her phone.

"I wanted to talk to you about what happened."

Women could be cruel. He knew that she had bailed on him when he had been in the hospital, and part of him didn't blame her. It was a lot to take after a first date. But they had been friends before they had been…involved. It was wrong to bail on a friend.

"Listen, I get it. It was too much. I don't want to rehash everything."

She stopped fidgeting then. "I would like to explain myself."

Inwardly, he sighed. He had dreamed of this. In those first few days in the hospital, he had prayed that she would show up and apologize. The need to forgive, to accept whatever she said, burned at the back of his throat. He swallowed.

"I don't see a reason to. I'm not in the mood to go through it. Not right now, not when I just got back. Let's just go with what we agreed. It was six months ago and better forgotten."

She stared at him, and for a second, he thought she might start crying. Her clear hazel eyes clouded before she slipped her mirrored sunglasses back on. He knew better. Catherine Kalakau didn't cry.

"Sure. Okay. See you later."

She turned and hurried in the direction of parking lot. He couldn't help but enjoy her pavement eating stride. The woman definitely knew how to cover a lot of ground fast.

He wanted to go after her and apologize. He had been harsh and he shouldn't have done that no matter what. But, he didn't. After watching her disappear around the corner, he shoved his hands into his pockets and then turned to go home. There was no reason to visit old wounds. A clean break is what they both needed.

Charity watched as TJ went back to the food truck to get another water. The man definitely knew how to move. And those legs. She sighed.

"Hey, Earth to Charity."

She glanced at Drew. "Sorry."

He shook his head. "No worries. He seems like a really nice guy."

"He is."

"I just..."

Then he trailed off. He looked at TJ, who was standing behind a family of four ordering. Drew glanced back at Charity. "I'm worried about you."

"Why?"

He hesitated for a long moment before speaking. "You don't act like this about other guys."

She nodded. She couldn't deny the fact that she had let him move in with her under the guise of protection, but knowing full well it would lead to the bedroom.

"Maybe that's a good thing."

"Yeah, but from someone who got trampled on not too long ago, take it from me. When it fails, it hurts. A lot. I think for the first time you might really get hurt."

And that was sad because she knew Drew was right. She had never been tempted to be hurt, to take a chance on someone. With everything that was going on with the investigation, it wasn't probably that smart to do.

"Don't you think it's a good thing? Like I'm growing or something?"

The sad smile Drew offered did little to help the way her heart quivered. She knew he had been hurt, but she thought he had moved on from it.

"I guess you'll just have to find out."

There was something in his tone that drew her attention. "Did something happen today?"

He hesitated, then looked out over to Kam Highway. Cars filled with tourists and locals, buzzed by. "Cat stopped me today. Wanted to talk about our issues."

"Is that what she called it?"

He shook his head. "She said she wanted to explain herself."

"What did you say?"

"I told her there was no reason for it."

The dead flat tone of his voice shocked her. "Drew."

He looked at her. "I thought about it, but she has had six months and a whole week of work. It was her idea to not discuss it. She's the one who decided we should just move on. I did what she asked, and she apparently expected me to do something different. She needs to learn to live with disappointment. I did."

Before she could respond, TJ returned to the table.

"Here you go," he said, handing them each their second water. "I'm a man who likes spicy food, and I will say that was definitely spicy."

Drew smiled and thanked him for the drink. Charity wanted to push, to get Drew to talk more about what happened, but the moment was over. She made a mental note to push later. Drew might think he was doing fine now that he was back at work. But he wasn't. Not by a long shot.

After breakfast at the Wailana Coffee House Saturday morning, TJ suggested they stop by his house in Waimanalo.

"I need to pick up some more clothes."

She shrugged, happy to go along. She was definitely interested in seeing his house. The ride took a little longer, as it was Saturday morning. Folks were heading to the beach since the waves were up on the other side of the island, but Charity didn't mind. She was in a Jeep without the roof, the sun was shining, and she was getting to know TJ. Right now, she didn't even want to think about work or Foley. She just wanted to be with TJ and pretend they were a normal couple.

By the time they made it there, she was definitely ready for a tour. He pulled into the driveway and parked the car. The street was quiet and definitely on it's way back. She knew this area had been hit hard by the ICE epidemic in years past, but refurbished homes and the presences of families told her those days were over.

It wasn't that big, but most houses in Hawaii were not big —at least on Oahu. Land space was limited and getting worse by the day. Real estate on the most populous of the islands was a nightmare. It fit the area and the size of land that surrounded it.

The house was painted green with white trim, pretty common in the islands. It was built in the fashion of a plantation house. Back home, they called it a farm house. The walk led up to a large, covered lanai, which boasted tons of planted pots and a swing attached to the roof. He had a little garden along the front lanai. A large banyan tree gave much of the small yard shade.

"What?' he asked as she stood there and stared.

"It's so cute."

"Don't sound surprised."

She glanced at him. "This is the crack house?"

He shook his head and waved to one of his neighbors, as they walked up the sidewalk to the lanai.

"It was when I bought it. I spent a weekend picking up discarded syringes, pipes, and spoons. And, it didn't even have a roof. Add in rats and a rotted floor, and it was definitely a fixer upper."

He unlocked the front door and stepped aside to let her enter. Lord, it was gorgeous.

"Is this wood?" she asked as she slipped off her sandals.

"Bamboo floors. More sustainable."

She smiled, then turned. "Oh, my word."

"They installed it yesterday."

Gray cabinets filled the walls, some with open shelving, some with glass doors. A farm house sink sat beneath a window she knew looked out over the lanai. It was still missing a stove and refrigerator, but she was already in love.

"The rest of the appliances are coming in a couple weeks. There was a delay."

It was perfect. At first look, the colors were bland. But when she took in the entire scene, she saw the beauty of it. Every little aspect complimented the others. She could imagine he would add pops of color after he was done.

"I love it."

He smiled. "I had to make sure that I had it ready by the end of next month."

"Why?"

"My parents are coming over. I'd like you to meet them."

"Your parents?" she asked, her voice coming out kind of strangled. He had taken her by surprise.

"Is there something wrong?"

"Under the circumstances, don't you think we should wait?"

His face softened, as he slipped his arms around her waist and pulled her closer. "We'll have this all cleared up by then."

"So, you plan on sticking around?"

"Sweetheart, you better believe it."

She released a breath she didn't know she had been holding. Meeting the parents. It was something she hadn't done in years, and she hadn't been sure she wanted to. Not until he mentioned it. Now, she was both terrified and excited by the prospect.

"Now, when you look like that, you worry me."

She sighed. "I've rarely had a serious relationship, and even more rarely, met my lover's family."

"Hey, you have time," he said, leaning down and nibbling on her bottom lip. "Plus, I'm sure my mom will have swag from Comic Con."

She placed a hand on his chest and pushed him back. "Don't you even be joking about that, Thor."

"Cross my heart."

"Well, then, I might be able to handle that."

He smiled and stepped back. Taking her hand, he tugged

her to a hallway off the kitchen. "Let me show you the rest of the house, especially the bedroom."

"Yeah?"

"I want your opinion on this bed I have."

She chuckled and followed him along. She'd worry about parents and relationships later.

The call at three in the morning caught Adam completely off guard. With his job, he was used to it, and he had a few younger cousins who often needed a ride after drinking too much on a Friday, but getting a call from Queen's Medical in the middle of the night stopped his heart.

It took him forty minutes to get there. He rushed into the ER, and used his badge to get passed all security. His cousin, Miyako—the person who had called him— met him in the hallway.

"She's going to be all right," she said.

The rock that had been planted in his chest since the moment he got the call let up. "What happened?"

"Overdose. Not sure if it was on purpose or accidental. Either way, she almost didn't make it." She studied him for a long minute. "You need to get her some help, and you need to let go."

Adam nodded. It wasn't anything he hadn't heard from friends and family in the last few months. But they didn't understand that wrapped in all his feelings for her, the biggest was guilt. Jin—no woman—should have suffered what she did.

"And you should call her family."

Constant Craving

"She has no one. Only child, both parents gone."

Miyako glanced at the door, then back at him. "Damn."

For the two of them, it was a hard thing to fathom. Their family was large and had its tentacles in about every facet on the island. Of course, there was only one point five degrees of separation between people on the islands, especially if you had even a drop of Hawaiian blood in you. To think that Jin had no one in the world was a little astounding.

"Thanks for the call."

"Anytime at all, cuz," she said as her name was called. She rolled her eyes. "Another day in paradise with the job I love."

She hurried off to answer the summons. Adam drew in a deep breath, trying his best to get his mind settled before walking through the door. He stared at his reflection in the glass. For months now, every time he got a midnight call, he had expected this. She had been bent on destruction, especially these last few weeks. But somehow, as horrible as he had thought it would be, it was a hundred times worse.

When he thought he was prepared, he slid the door and curtain aside. They had left the lights low, except for a small light illuminating the bed. Jin laid there, her face pale, dark circles under her eyes. She was so still, it surprised Adam she was still breathing. She had lost weight...a lot. She had never been a skinny woman, but now her skin hung on her. Her cheeks were hollow. If he could see her eyes, he knew they would be void of the light he had always loved.

Adam settled in the seat by her bed and took her hand. There were fine lined scars marring her light brown skin. She might have healed physically, but there would always be reminders of that week she had lived in hell—not to mention nightmares.

"Adam," she murmured.

He looked up, but her eyes were still closed. In sleep, she would turn to him, she would accept him. It was enough for right now. When she was cleared, he would make her go get help, or he would have to walk away. There was no way around that. Adam couldn't keep riding the emotional rollercoaster. It had to end soon.

With no other answers, Adam held onto her hand and bent his head to pray.

Chapter Fifteen

Late Sunday morning, TJ was in the shower, and Charity was getting ready to make pancakes for them when her cell buzzed. The moment she saw the number, she made a face. She loved her family, but she was no good at lying to them. If she wasn't careful, her mother would figure out there was something wrong. She would then tell Charity's father, and they would be there within a day. She did not need the family drama at her doorstep. But, if she avoided her mother, she would become even more suspicious. Charity clicked on the phone.

"Hey, Mama, how's it going?"

"Not well. Your father found out about your grandparents."

Luke was purring and rubbing up against her legs. She bent down and picked him up to nuzzle him. "How did that happen?"

"It was kind of hard to miss since your grandfather moved in with your grandmother."

Charity blinked as the ability to think dissolved. "What?"

"You heard me. Your grandfather is living up at the big house."

"Who are you talking to?" her father said in the background.

"Your daughter. Catching her up."

"Gimme," her father said.

The phone was handed over to her father. "Hey, baby, how are you doing today?"

"Fine. Just getting ready to make some pancakes."

"Sour cream pancakes?"

"Yes."

"Your mother won't let me eat them that often."

"Your cholesterol was high last time you went to the doc."

"She's even turned you against me. Even your grandmother questions my food choices."

She smiled. "She loves you."

"At the moment, that doesn't count for much. Your mother said you knew."

"I thought maybe she had started smoking crack."

Her father sighed. "Yeah, well, maybe your grandparents have."

She leaned against the counter. Her father sounded confused and not all that angry. At least not any more. She knew he had a temper, but it was burned out quickly.

"Did you talk to them?"

"Yeah," he said.

"And? What did they say?" she asked, as TJ came walking into the kitchen. His hair was damp, and he was wearing a pair of board shorts. Damn, she should have joined him in the shower.

Of course, Luke—the traitor—slipped out of her grasp to

go see TJ. Jess—the other defector—was trailing after TJ as if she were in love.

"They said life is too short to waste it alone."

"Sounds like they have the right state of mind."

"It's still weird."

"Daddy, our family has always been weird."

"This takes it up another notch."

She laughed, as TJ stepped behind her and slipped his arms around her waist. He started to nibble on her neck.

"True. Did you yell at them?"

"Yes. And I left."

She rolled her eyes. Knowing her father, he would make up with the grandparents today.

"So, what are you up to, baby?"

"A little of this and a little of that."

"And you can't talk to me about it."

"Not while the investigation is active." And one where your baby is being set up. That would be a disaster. He would show up with expensive investigators and start messing things up and pissing off not only the FBI but probably Del.

"Okay. Well, your mother is on the landline, and I have feeling it's your grandmother. I guess I have to go talk to her."

"Yeah, that would be good."

"Love you, buttercup."

"Love ya."

She clicked off the phone, and TJ spun her around and kissed her. When he pulled back, her head was spinning, and she was out of breath.

"I was going to make breakfast."

He took her hand and tugged her toward the bedroom. "After."

She smiled and went willingly. They definitely had time for breakfast later.

An hour later, they were finally sitting down to breakfast. TJ eyed the massive stack of sour cream pancakes Charity set in front of him and smiled.

"Now, this I could get used to."

Charity chuckled. "Hey, I believe you earned it this morning.

She placed maple syrup and coconut syrup on the table. "I think I did, although, I think I got more pleasure out of it than you did."

She just smiled and grabbed her own plate to join him.

"How about we go to the beach?" he asked.

"That actually sounds good. If you think it's okay."

TJ nodded. "We're supposed to be acting normal. We could ask Drew to go too."

"You don't have to do that."

He looked up at her and smiled. "But I want to. I think getting out is good for him."

Charity beamed at him, and he felt as if he had done something spectacular...like cured cancer. And that is all it took. He had found out through that weekend that making her happy was a priority. He had always been taught to think of others, but he had never had so much resting on one individual. It was troublesome. He was getting tangled up in her, but that is what a guy did, right? They got caught up in a woman when they fell in love.

The whole idea that he was in love with her was still

bothering him, but there wasn't anything he really could do about it. Fighting it was going to be insanely hard, especially since he had to stick to her.

He dug into his pancakes and sighed. The woman could definitely cook. It wasn't a prerequisite for him when it came to women, as he could fend for himself, but it was nice to have someone make breakfast for him. Even nicer to have breakfast with someone.

"What do you think about being tourists and heading to Waikiki?" Charity suggested.

He swallowed his bite of pancake and nodded. "I've really only been there once. On the beach that is."

"I don't go that often. Waimanalo is my favorite."

He nodded. "It's one of the reasons I had looked for a house over there."

When he had taken her to his house the day before, part of it was to get his clothes. The other part was to show off a little bit. No one other than contractors had been in his house. He hadn't really clicked with anyone since moving to the islands—that is until he met the members of TFH. They didn't seem to think twice about welcoming him into their lives. Well, after they checked him out.

What he hadn't expected was that Charity would look so right in his house. He could see her working in the kitchen, or curled up on a chair in the screened-in lanai working on her laptop. Now that he had seen her there, it was hard to get the image out of his head.

"TJ?"

"Oh, sorry. My mind was drifting."

"Nothing on Foley, I guess? Nothing on why the FBI has messed up video?"

He shook his head.

"I hate that this is moving so slowly." The frustration was easy to hear in her voice. "It's one of the reasons I left the CIA."

"What?"

"The federal government. I was always going to be working for government. My expertise is for investigation, so it was either teach or work in government. I don't mind teaching a course every now and then; but long term, I would burn my eyeballs out."

"You work for the government here."

She shook her head. "It's different. We move faster because the cases we have are all top priority. We are set up to move at an accelerated pace. I don't have to wait for this supervisor, or that appointed committee chair approval. I go to Del. Del fixes it. This situation is annoying."

He set down his fork and took her hand. "Hey. We'll get it all worked out."

She smiled at him again. "I know."

As they finished up breakfast, TJ realized that he was having issues with the pace of the investigation too. It was annoying, and he was not a man who had a problem with long, slow investigations. In fact, it was considered his fortes. He was known for digging beneath the surface and closing every loophole. Most of his cases were settled before court because the evidence was irrefutable. Now though, two weeks into the investigation and he wanted it done. And there was one reason for that.

He wanted to get on with his life—and Charity. As the investigation hung over their heads, they couldn't do more than just what had been going on. Dating, not mentioning the future. He had a feeling that Charity didn't go for deep relationships, but he wanted more. He wanted some kind of direction, and he wanted to know that this was more than just the investigation.

Until they were done, he wouldn't know if it was just about the situation or there is something more.

Charity enjoyed the soft breeze Sunday afternoon. She and TJ, and now their new sidekick Drew, were at the beach. She thought when she had moved to Hawaii she would spend at least every weekend at the beach. She loved the smell of the salt water, sunscreen, and fresh flowers. But, after a few months, she found herself like a lot of other residents. Work took priority and sometimes, just sometimes, she resented the fact that she had to work and not play every weekend. And it made her hate tourists.

So, when TJ had suggested they go to the beach over breakfast, she had been happy to accommodate. Instead of going all the way down to the main beach area of Waikiki, they opted for the spot in front of the Hale Koa. It could get just as crowded, but there were less kids in this area. Plus, they had walked, and Charity just wanted to sit and relax. This was closer.

TJ spread his beach towel out, then took hers.

"Hey, I can handle that."

He just smiled. He was wearing a t-shirt that said *Nerd? I prefer the term intellectual badass* –which Drew had loved. TJ set her towel beside his, then peeled that shirt off. Good lord, the man was built. Not big muscles, but those long, lean muscles swimmers had. Then there was that little trail of golden hair that lead down and disappeared into his trunks.

"Stop drooling. It's disgusting," Drew said.

She smiled. "I can always appreciate a beautiful male body."

He shook his head and took off his shirt. The scars on his chest had faded, but they were still there. Would always be there. One thin line bisected his pecs, an ugly reminder of getting shot and dying—if only for a few seconds. Then she realized he was a little more bulked up.

"Have you been working out?" she asked.

"Physical therapy," Drew said as he slipped on his goggles and grabbed his board.

"Are you supposed to be surfing?"

He tossed her a nasty look and trudged out to the water.

"You sound like his mom," TJ said.

"Do I?"

He nodded.

"You weren't around then. It was scary."

He nodded. "But he's not a boy. He might be a dork or a nerd, but he's a man, and he can handle himself. I think he'd do better if you would quit hovering."

She slid her glasses down on her nose. "Is that a fact?"

He shook his head and leaned down for a quick kiss. "Don't get that tone. I think being out on his own is good for him. He might have doubted himself after the shooting."

"And just why do you know better than I do?"

"First, because I've been shot, and I know the doubts that can creep in. It makes it worse that Cat abandoned him."

"She might have her reasons."

"You really do have a soft heart. I can also see things

because I wasn't here, and so I wasn't affected by all of it. He's going to be fine, Charity. He's a good man and he has good friends."

Then he made his way to the water. She watched him go, knowing he was right. Drew *was* doing better now, and he did look a lot lighter. The darkness that had been hanging over him seemed to have lifted a little. Drew was taking the initiative to go out. He had told her that he was meeting with some old friends next weekend. Just hearing that had made her happy.

And, of course, TJ had noticed it. She hated that the man was right, and did it by giving her a compliment. It made him even sweeter. She sat down on her towel and sighed.

How was she not supposed to fall for a man like that?

Charity had one motto for Mondays. They sucked. The only good Monday was one spent on vacation, in her opinion. This Monday was no different. Charity hung up her cell and stared out at her lab.

Thieving, dirty bastard.

Drew came walking into her lab, then stopped in his tracks.

"Uh-oh. Who is going to die?"

Irritation didn't cover it, but Drew showing up before she could contain herself was problematic for her. She wasn't someone who held in her emotions, but she knew when she was ready to kill. Just like her father, she could lash out and hurt people just because they were in the vicinity. Today was one of those days.

"I figured out what the bastard is going to do to me. Is Emma upstairs?"

Drew nodded, as he followed her out of the lab and up the stairs. They reached the second floor, and she went in search of Emma, Drew keeping up with her.

They found Emma in the boss' office.

"Hey. So, I just had a call from my bank."

"Yeah?" Del asked.

"Someone tried to book a first class ticket to the UAE in my name. *One way*."

There was a moment of stunned silence. The first one to speak was Del. "What the hell? Did they let them buy the ticket?"

"No. They stopped it, thank goodness. I have a really good bank, and they pay attention to things like that. Completely out of character for me."

"He was trying to set you up," Emma said. "And the United Arab Emirates has no extradition policy with the US."

Charity nodded. "So, it made it look like I was trying to go there. But to what end? Nothing has been stolen. Sure someone tried to hack into the system, but no big job had been pulled. A few identities were stolen, but the hack was so damned clumsy, they had time to contact the operatives. Nothing else has happened," Charity said. "It feels as if we are on some snipe hunt."

"What are snipes?" Emma asked.

Del smiled. "Imaginary animals."

Emma looked at Charity. "Why would you hunt an imaginary animal? Oh, wait. Got it."

"I know what you are saying. And now messing with

your credit," Del said. "This makes it feel as if they are painting you as the bad person. You will be left holding the bag and be accused of all the wrongdoing. You wouldn't get charged, but it would keep everyone busy until he slipped away."

"And nothing big. Just something that would divert attention to me. But to what end? The only thing I can think of is that the bastard is trying to get the FBI to chase their tails while they do what they want to do."

"Even if they are doing anything at all," Emma said.

"What do you mean?"

"Maybe this is just it. This game of messing with you, keeping Remington, Callahan, the rest of the FBI busy."

Drew rocked back on his heels. "There is a good chance that is it. While they didn't catch Foley, they did make it harder for him to make money selling secrets. That had to piss him off."

"And it could be payback, but it just doesn't feel that is the only purpose," Charity said.

"Have you told TJ about the credit card stuff?" Drew asked.

"No. I just got off the phone with my bank about it when you walked into my lab. I only had time to pick out what instrument to use on the bastard."

"Whoa, what did I miss?" TJ asked.

They all turned to face him. She hadn't expected him to show up this early in the day. His presence was a soothing balm to her agitated nerves. Still, Emma's personality must have rubbed off on her.

"What are you doing here?"

He chuckled. "Well, that's a sweet welcome."

"We have a situation here," Drew said.

She internally sighed. Since Friday night, Drew had softened toward TJ. Sunday at the beach had solidified his friendship with TJ. She just hoped when all this was over, TJ and he stayed friendly. She wasn't sure where they were going, but right now in Drew's life, he needed people who would be there to back him up.

"What happened?" TJ asked his smile fading.

"Someone was messing with my credit. Trying to make it look like I plan to flee the country."

She explained what happened and what they thought about it.

"Well, one thing I know is that it isn't Foley. Especially if it was done in the last twenty-four hours."

"Why do you say that?" Del asked.

"Because, according to the FBI and Europol, Edward Foley is dead."

Chapter Sixteen

The stunned silence that filled Del's office didn't surprise TJ. The ticking of the clock was the only sound in an otherwise rowdy office. It was a little eerie. Of course, that had been the same reaction he'd had when he'd gotten the notice just a half hour earlier.

"Do you want to repeat that again?" Del asked, carefully annunciating every word.

"He's dead, or at least a man with his fingerprints is dead."

Del shook his head, then stood. "Call everyone in. We need to do this all at once. I need all hands on deck."

Drew had his phone out before Del was done talking. TJ forced himself to look at Charity. For the first time since he had known her, there was no expression on her face. He didn't know what more to say.

"Dead, dead?" she asked.

He couldn't get a read on her, and that was troublesome. He would say she was shocked, but that might be an understatement. Truth is, he would rather she be furious.

He shrugged. "I'll go over it all when everyone gets here, but I will say that I'm not convinced it is the man. You should have a report by now. It went out to all the agencies on the island."

"That's not normal," she said frowning.

"I'm sure it isn't, but it's the way I do things. Or, at least, the way I do them now."

She smiled. "Yeah?"

"Of course, it makes sense," Emma said, pushing herself out of her seat. He wasn't sure, but she looked like she had grown in size just since he had seen her the day before. "You sent it out to all the agencies who have cyber crime units, which is everywhere these days. That way, we can have the info without alerting whoever is doing this. You didn't single us out, and you didn't break any rules. You're smart."

Emma spoke to him like she was his mother. "Thanks."

"For a fed."

Charity chuckled, as Emma and Del left the office.

"Did she just insult me?"

She shook her head. "No. That is high praise from Emma."

"Not very high when she says fed in the same tone people use for Ebola."

She smiled, but it didn't reach her eyes. He studied her for a long second. He knew there was something wrong. Outside of everything else that was happening, something had happened since he had seen her off to work that morning. "What happened?"

She blinked. "What?"

"You looked distressed when I came in. In fact, you were

talking about hurting people, so I know there is something off."

"You got that from just looking at me?"

TJ shoved his hands into his pockets. It was hard to explain to the woman he loved—especially since she didn't know he was in love with her—that he would always be able to look at her and tell when something was wrong.

"Yeah. Something happened this morning before I showed up."

"Oh, that. Someone tried to hack into my accounts. They were using them for one way tickets, or tried to. My bank put a stop to it."

Something cold danced over the fine hairs of his neck. It sent a chill racing down his spine and into his blood. "Don't brush it off."

"It's pretty commonplace."

"Yes, and that's why people report it to their bank and then go from there. But, it's so simple, it could be part of the plot to frame you."

She frowned and studied him for a moment. "But you said Foley was dead."

He shook his head, as he started to think what had happened in the last few hours. "We can't dismiss it. And we don't know for sure he was Foley, or if it is just one person. We always thought it was, because of a set of fingerprints at one of the murders, but I can't rule out that it's a team."

She sighed, then nodded. He hated the expression on her face. She felt as if she had done something wrong, that somehow she should have prevented what was going on. She had done nothing to put herself in this situation.

"It's going to turn out okay."

"You think?" she asked.

He stepped closer and slipped his hand into hers. "Hey, you have a kick ass team, and one hell of an FBI agent to help you. The bastard behind this doesn't stand a chance. We'll figure out what the hell is going on."

Drawing in a deep breath, then releasing it slowly, she nodded. The smile she gave him this time was genuine.

"Come on. I'm going to pull up the report someone at the FBI sent."

He followed her out, and noticed that the team members were making their way in. They weren't a big force, but they were a strong one. It was something he had been missing since he had gotten here, that *Ohana* feeling everyone talked about in Hawaii. They had it here in TFH, and, as Del took his seat, he realized they had adopted him—at least for the moment.

He glanced at Charity, who was tapping on the laptop pulling up the memo he had sent out. It came up on the screen.

"They say the fingerprints match," she said.

"Yes, but not much else. We know that the real Foley knows how to get people to fix things like that," he said. "Plus, Foley wasn't his real name, or assumed it wasn't. This man was living under the name, but I have a feeling that this isn't the man at the top."

"Why?" Del asked.

"As I said, Foley was made up. It wasn't a real name. So, it would make sense he picks some idiot, slaps the name on him, then kills him when things heat up."

"He would be that coldblooded?" Graeme asked.

TJ nodded. "Money is his main objective. If this isn't the

man we think is Foley, he's just someone the real criminal used."

"Oh," Charity said.

"What?" he asked. When he looked at her, she was on her computer.

"Something just popped up. His name wasn't Foley. It was Jacob Heller, and he was an accountant at the FBI."

"Another tie to the FBI," Emma said. "Sounds like your house is quite a mess over there, Callahan."

He didn't disagree with her. For the last year, he had regretted ever being assigned to the Foley case. He had been growing obsessive with it before the shooting. When he saw his chance, he walked away. But now, he was thinking that might have been a mistake. He was FBI, but he also knew that not everyone in the FBI was a good person. A lot of agents didn't want to admit that. By heading off to Hawaii, he might have allowed Foley to expand his influence and get someone in his old department to help. "We never thought Foley was his real name."

"But here's my main problem with it," Charity said. "Someone tried to buy tickets with my bank account. A place with no extradition treaty with the US. The UAE is very particular about letting the US government take people."

"None of this is making sense. What is the man after at this point?" Adam asked.

"That's a good question," Charity said. "Right now, I can't understand why I would be singled out. No identities were stolen, right?"

"No. No cover ops were revealed, just someone tried to get in. Even if they did get the information, they didn't act on it."

"Please. There would be no *try* if I wanted to get that information."

"Charity, I try my best to pretend we are on the up and up, and you say this in front of the fed," Del admonished.

"Nothing but the truth," TJ said, smiling.

"Thank you, sir."

"It's a set up," Emma said.

Charity shrugged. "We knew that from the beginning though. Foley was going to use me as the fall guy on this job."

"No, this is different," Emma said, turning to TJ. "Right?"

He was already starting to think. It was different. Foley had never been caught so early and in such a way that would have them actively looking for him. Before, they always seemed to be three moves behind him. Now it seemed he was signaling each move.

"He changed it up this time."

Foley's MO had always been that he would use someone, connect with them. Then, he would kill them, or leave them to pay the price. It now felt as if Charity was the person in question.

"It's a different kind of set up," he said.

"His final set up," Emma commented, and he nodded again.

"What do you..." Charity frowned and looked down at her computer. "This is odd."

"What?" He leaned over her shoulder and saw an email from Jacob Heller. "Don't open it."

She looked at him, then back at the screen. "You think it might be a virus?"

"Or another trap of some sort. Leave it alone and we'll deal with it."

She nodded. "I'll run a check on it. Emma can help me with that, right? Either way, whoever this is is trying to make it look like I'm involved."

"You're Foley," Emma said.

"What?" Charity asked.

A sense of dread coursed through him, as he started really listening to Emma. She wasn't piecing it all together at once, but now it was hitting him what it might mean.

"You're Foley," TJ said.

Charity looked at him, then to Emma, then back at him. The expression on her face told TJ she thought they had both lost their minds.

"I am not Foley."

"But he's trying to make it look like you are," Drew said shaking his head. "I don't know why I didn't see it before."

"And making me look like Foley does what?"

"When did the problems with Foley start? Not now with Charity but overall?" Emma asked.

"Dammit. Three years ago, when you were at CIA, Charity."

"But I never had a hand in it."

"He wanted someone like you. Someone with connections on the island—for what reason, I don't understand. He needed someone who had an association with DC, but not with the FBI. Your time at the CIA was perfect. Your reputation as a hacker helped out even more. He could be fixing you up to be the fall woman for his final job."

Before she could respond, TJ's phone buzzed. He looked down and saw Remington's number.

"Damn."

"What?"

"It's Remington." He turned off his phone. "There's something really off about all of this."

"What do you mean?" she asked.

"Listen, more than likely, that was Remington calling to say they found a link between you and Heller. That was too fast. Someone has to be feeding him information."

"And you turned your phone off, why?" Adam asked.

"I don't want to answer and ping off a cell tower here. I also disabled the GPS."

"They let you do that?" Charity asked.

"My personal phone. I left the work phone back at the office."

"So, we think that the bastard is trying to stack the deck against Charity," Adam said. "Buy why?"

"He's done."

They all turned to look at Emma.

"What do you mean?" Del asked.

"This guy is done. He's going to take all the money he has earned and ride off into the sunset."

"It isn't that much money, is it?" Marcus asked.

"Over four billion estimated," TJ said. "That is our estimate on how much he made off of selling secrets. Lord only knows what else he did."

"But he might not be disappearing forever. Just reinventing himself. This identity has gotten too hot, so he kills himself off, produces another frame job, then poof, he's gone. I'll be left holding the proverbial bag," Charity said.

"You won't though."

She glanced up at him. "Is that a fact?"

"Bet on it."

She nodded. "So, what do we do now?"

Constant Craving

"I need to head back to the office, get hold of Remington. We need to find out where that email came from."

"We can handle that," Charity said. "I'm an expert, but Emma outranks me."

"Of course I do. I have a genius IQ, and it isn't a title like they give to the people who work in the Apple stores, either," Emma said.

"Are you sure? You have to make sure you don't let it get into your computer."

She snorted. "I think you have just offended Emma and me."

He smiled, then leaned down to kiss her. "I'll call as soon as I hear anything."

She nodded. Del rose. "I'll walk you out."

Damn, that sounded ominous.

"No problem."

Drew watched as Callahan and Del walked out the door.

"Oh, I hope he doesn't go all big brother on TJ. He had to know we were involved," Charity said.

Emma shrugged. "Like it or not, he sees himself as the patriarch of the TFH family."

"I don't even want to think about what they are talking about. Wanna go to my lab to work?"

Emma nodded.

"See y'all later."

As soon as they turned the corner, money started exchanging hands. "So, who had the bet on Callahan and Charity, and when did it exactly happen?" Graeme asked.

They all looked at Drew. "Hey, I don't know when they started sleeping together."

"But they *are* sleeping together, right?" Cat asked.

"Yeah, from the way they were acting this past weekend, I would say yes."

"Elle, you're holding that bet, right? I think until we get date confirmation, we don't do anything," Cat said.

She nodded. "And, I call today as the day to pick the birthday of the first TFH baby. She is due exactly a month from today. Oh, and who is going to ask Charity the date?"

Again, they all looked at him. "I am not asking one of my best friends when she bagged the agent."

"Emma is your best bet to ask rude questions like that," Graeme said. "And everyone let's her get away with it."

"I'll talk to Emma later, ask her to ask Charity," Elle said. "This shuts down the baby pool."

"I have seen none of this, but you have my bet, right?" Adam said.

Elle nodded. "All we have to do is wait."

TJ slipped his sunglasses on, as they stepped out of the building. Del did the same thing. He glanced at the commander. He knew Martin Delano's background. Former special forces, chest full of medals, and now head of the Task Force Hawaii. All that he knew from reports. But, in the last few weeks, he had seen that he was more. If TFH was a family, this was the head of it.

"So, is this where you take me out behind the building and beat the shit out of me?"

Del glanced at him and waited until some people passed by them

"No. Charity has many hidden talents, and one of those is being able to take care of herself."

"So, this talk is about what?"

"In a round about way, it is about the same thing."

"Damn, I thought FBI people were good at code. Yours is so cryptic, I have no fucking idea what you're talking about."

The smile came fast and dissolved faster. "First, if things go wrong, you don't really have to worry about physical harm."

At first, TJ smiled, thinking he was joking. Del just stared at him. "Well, that's good because the FBI usually doesn't like it when their agents are threatened."

"Emma will just ruin you financially if you hurt Charity."

"What?"

"Sorry, but my wife lost her family a few years ago, and she sees Charity as part of her *Ohana*. Emma will ruin you if you intentionally hurt her."

"Okay."

"Just like that?"

TJ shrugged. "My family can be a little cut throat also."

Del nodded. "Now, the other thing I want to talk to you about is your job. This might put it in jeopardy."

That much was true, but he had never thought about that. Not really. When he realized Charity was innocent, he couldn't let her get caught up in something she had nothing to do with. Before, he might have gone to higher ups and fought his position, but with Charity, he would give everything up to protect her.

"I know that part of it is worth it for you. Charity is a special woman."

"I know that."

"Yes, I see that, but I think you might be special to her. See, men don't last long with Charity."

"We haven't been going out that long."

"But for Charity, it is. Men rarely last long with her because she gets bored. Or they ask for more than she wants to give them. The fact that you are still hanging around tells me you're different. She feels something for you, and don't get me wrong, I know you feel something for her. But I want to make sure you're doing this for the right reasons outside of your relationship with Charity."

"She's enough of a reason."

Del nodded. "Yeah, but take it from someone who fell in love with his wife while working a case, some of the feelings you have for her will be wrapped up in this case. You need to make sure that after this case, if you should go your separate ways, that you did this for other reasons."

"I thought you were her friend."

"I am, and she cares about you. Why are you doing this, other than for Charity?"

She was the most important part, but from the start of it, there had been something off. "It's not right."

"No. But that doesn't always get people to act."

"True. Still, I don't like this kind of investigation. Remington used to be good. Really good. But, this case messed with his head, and he started seeing problems with everyone. Everyone could be a suspect. When Charity popped up on the screen, she had to be a dream come true. Remington had always theorized there was someone in the federal government helping. This would prove it. That means that Foley knows him well, and probably picked out Charity because she would appeal to his theories."

"And you disagree."

"Oh, no, I agree, but I don't think CIA. They could do it, but I'm not sure they would do it as well as someone on the inside. Let's be honest, there is a good chance CIA agent lists could fetch a bigger payday than FBI. So, I always thought FBI. Remington just didn't want it to be our organization. The fact that he already knows Heller emailed Charity makes me think Foley may not just have an inside man, he might *be* the inside man. Someone no one would suspect."

"Okay. Just be careful out there. With this ramping up of emails and stolen credit, we will definitely keep an eye on her."

"Thanks."

"Oh, and just so you know, you don't have to worry about me or any of the men hurting you. The TFH women might not just ruin your credit if you hurt her. Cat's a black belt, and Elle's had defensive training. Emma could definitely beat the shit out of you if she wasn't pregnant."

He thought of Del's petite wife and chuckled. "I find that hard to believe."

Del shook his head. "She lived on the streets in Thailand from the time she was sixteen. I have personal experience with her ability to protect herself. She wouldn't think twice about hurting someone who hurt her *Ohana*."

He knew from Del's tone of voice, he might be joking, but there was an underlying message: Don't fuck with the women of TFH.

"I'll keep that in mind."

Chapter Seventeen

An hour later, Charity, Emma, and Drew were in her office as she prepared to open the email. They had done every kind of possible test before they opened it. There were no attachments, no bugs within the email that they could detect, and they had an early warning system ready to go if it should start to download anything.

"This makes me a little sick to my stomach," Drew said.

Charity glanced at him, then back to her laptop screen. "I know what you mean. Every time I think I'm ready to open in, my stomach starts doing somersaults. I'm regretting those pancakes this morning."

"I'm hungry."

They both looked at Emma. Her eyes were closed as she rubbed her belly.

"You're always hungry these days," Charity said.

She smiled as she opened her eyes. "Butch takes a lot of food."

"Butch?"

"Del didn't want to know the sex of the baby, so we are going with Butch for right now."

"Do you know?" Drew asked.

Emma smiled.

Charity chuckled. "Does Del know you know?"

"No. We had a huge fight at Dr. Gregory's last time we were there. I was so irritated with him, I might have said disparaging things against the Seahawks, but I blame it on the hormones. They make me do silly things. Besides, it's a dumbass move not to use what science has given us, but then, I'm amazed he doesn't have a flip phone."

Something loosened in Charity's chest. The normalcy of Emma mocking Del—but not knowing she was actually mocking him—eased Charity's worries a little bit. It was so...normal.

Charity drew in a deep breath and released it slowly. Her heart was pounding so hard against her chest, she was sure both Emma and Drew could hear it. She blinked as the room revolved. Mentally, she counted down from ten to one, trying to get her nerves back under control. It was no big thing, just an email. Nothing like it could ruin her life forever.

With a less than steady finger, Charity pressed enter and waited for the alarms to sound.

It opened easily, no viruses, just a message.

Charity,

FBI on to me. You need to get to the UAE as soon as you can.

Heller

None of them said anything for a long moment. It was as if all of them were still holding their collective breaths waiting for the other shoe to drop. Then, Emma exploded.

"What the bloody hell does that mean?"

Charity shook her head. "I'm not really sure, but we know one thing. Our suspicions that whoever is behind this setting me up are dead on. But, why me? Why pick some forensic tech in Hawaii who had nothing to do with the FBI, other than to turn them down for a job? Or, well, take the CIA up on their offer before the FBI could pull their head's out of their asses long enough."

"Do you think it could be that?" Drew asked.

"What? That I worked for the CIA?"

"That you went to work for them instead of the FBI."

Charity snorted. "Not likely. I mean, it was years ago, and they really didn't pursue me. I had no other contact with the FBI before TJ."

Drew snorted. "So, that's what you're calling it?"

She gave him a warning look, but he just returned an innocent smile.

"I remember when you didn't like him at all," Charity said.

"You know, it may not be because of you picking the CIA over the FBI, but it definitely ties into your work there," Emma said.

"I had no cases open when I left DC. None. I cleared my work and made sure I tied up all the loose ends."

"But, you are cyber and you were there. In fact, outside of the federal government offices here on the island, you are probably the only former fed with that experience."

She shook her head. "There are others in the private sector."

"Ah, but they don't have access to things about Foley. The government has kept that close to their chests, and while a former fed working for a security agency here might know about Foley, access to the files he would want or need wouldn't work out. You also are a one-person forensic dynamite."

"That's true," Drew said. "You work mainly on your own. Someone who works for a security firm wouldn't have the freedom. And, there would always be someone looking over their shoulder. The overlords as you call them."

She nodded. "And that sets me up. Still, this feels personal, but why? I didn't really interview with anyone at the FBI. Not formally. And after I started working with the CIA, they didn't try to steal me away. They did that to one of my coworkers. So, why does this make me think I was targeted, but not by accident?"

"Of course you weren't targeted by accident," Drew said.

"What I mean is that he could have easily picked another forensic tech or computer expert anywhere. They picked Hawaii in particular. Is it me, or is there another agenda? But what the hell would that be?"

Emma smiled. "That is a brilliant observation. We haven't looked at why you would be picked. You haven't had any association with anyone from the FBI before this, right?"

Charity shook her head. "Not really. Just what I mentioned."

Emma started pacing, but it was more a duck waddle than her usual active pacing. "Is it personal to you? I mean, your family hasn't been attacked."

She thought about her present family issue and shook her head. "Nope, just strange bed partners."

"Yeah, what's going on with that?" Drew asked.

"They claim they are going to move in together. I am staying out of it."

He opened his mouth, but Emma stopped him. "No. Stop going off onto something else. We need to focus. We'll talk about the incest in Charity's family later."

"It isn't incest," Charity mumbled.

Emma smiled. "I know. I made a joke. Cool, huh?"

For Emma, it was an amazing feat. She had issues with sarcasm and humor, but had been working hard to learn the ins and outs of human interaction—as Emma called anything that made her uncomfortable.

She turned and paced away, then turned around. "Charity, we need to sit down and think of everything that has happened in the last month. Anything that might have been a ripple effect of this investigation, even before it started. Then, we might see something."

"That's an excellent idea," Charity said.

"Of course it is. I came up with it," Emma said with no humor, as she approached Charity's desk. Charity grabbed a pen and paper just as Emma let out a groan and gripped the side of the desk.

"Bloody hell."

"What's wrong?" Drew asked rushing to her side.

Emma's face drained of all color, and Charity was positive that the expectant mother was going to pass out. Charity jumped up and moved to slip her arm around Emma. The mother-to-be held up a hand to ward them both off.

"No," she said, breathing heavily. "I think we might need to get Del."

"Oh, hell," Charity said and grabbed her phone and hit the boss's number.

"What?" Drew asked looking from Emma to Charity.

Sometimes, she forgot how clueless Drew was when it came to the obvious. "She's in labor."

Drew took a step back. "Oh."

"Well, now we know how you'll handle fatherhood, Franklin," Emma said as she lowered herself to the chair.

Del answered on the second ring.

"What do you have?"

"I have your wife in my office, and she might be going into labor."

There was a short pause. "That's not funny."

"Do you hear me laughing?"

"She's not due for another month." He said it as if making the declaration made it true. Again, men. They always seemed to think everything ran on their schedule.

"Are you really arguing with me about whether or not Emma is in labor?"

"Oh, I am," Emma said. "I've been having contractions since about three this morning," Emma said.

Charity blinked and pulled the phone away from her ear. Del had heard what Emma said, and was yelling on the other end of the phone. He was so damned loud, all three of them could hear him.

"We'll get her up there."

She hung up as he continued to yell at her. She looked at Emma. "Let's go, woman. You're about to have a baby."

Emma didn't move to stand up. Instead, she shook her head.

"What?" Charity asked.

Emma looked at both she and Drew.

"I'm not ready," Emma confessed in a small voice.

Constant Craving

For the second time in about as many minutes, Charity blinked. "I don't think you have a choice. Babies decide when they are going to show up. And while I hate the stereotypes in *Gone with the Wind*, I will say, I don't know anything about birthing babies. We have to get you to the hospital."

"I don't like being on anyone else's schedule."

Charity laughed. "Oh, this is going to be fun. Neither does your husband, but I think you are both going to find out that things are about to change. Come on. Drew, get the door."

She helped Emma up out of the chair, and they walked to the elevator together. "I'm serious, Charity. I had another month to prepare. I have not mentally prepared for this. I'm not sure I'm going to be good at it."

"Good at what? Labor?"

Emma sighed and her eyes filled up. "Being a mom."

Charity was completely out of her depth. Most of her friends were men, and the women she knew weren't even thinking about having babies yet. She had never had to reassure anyone about something like this. Panic had her looking at Drew, who shook his head. He was going to be no help whatsoever. Men. Charity only knew one person who could have helped her, and that was her mother.

"My mother always thought she was the worst mom. Horrible. She was always worried she spoiled me, or that she was too hard on me. And, during my teen years especially, I thought she was. But, you know what? She's the best mom there is around. Every mother doubts she is good enough or strong enough. I would say that makes you damned normal. You have a great husband, your brother and his other people, and then you have us. We'll help you."

Emma nodded, but Charity could tell she wasn't convinced. She slipped her arm over her shoulders. "You're going to rock being a mom. Don't you worry. You're a genius, and that baby is probably going to be one too. You'll both do fine with Del by your side."

She wiped away the tears and smiled. "Yeah?"

"Yeah."

The elevator doors opened up and revealed an irritated Del. His usually easygoing attitude had been replaced with a thunderous frown.

"You've been having labor pains all day?" he bellowed.

Emma shrugged. "Just since this morning."

"This is the most asinine thing you have done." He hadn't lowered his voice one bit.

For a long second, she expected Emma to yell back. Charity knew the two of them were well-matched in that department. Instead, Emma burst into tears. For a moment, no one said anything. The look of terror on Del's face almost made Charity laugh. In the next instant, he snapped into action.

"I'm sorry, baby. Come on, the bag is in the truck. We'll get you to Queen's. I've already called Dr. Gregory. She's meeting us at the birthing center."

He slipped his arm around her and urged her onto the elevator.

"You two coming?" he asked.

"I have to shut things down in the lab. Then I'll follow."

"I need to check with Elle, then I'll be there too," Drew said.

Del nodded as the door closed.

"See ya in a few minutes. Want to ride together?"

Constant Craving

She shook her head. "I want to go over some stuff first." He hesitated, causing her to roll her eyes. "I'll call TJ and get him to bring me if no one else is around. Really, there is no physical threat to me, and especially in *this* building."

"Okay. But if you can't get him, you call me."

She nodded and waved him away. As she sat down at her desk again, she called TJ, but got his voice mail. She left him a message that she had opened the email and to call her back. Then, she started working on the list Emma had told her to make. Babies usually took time, and she wanted this done before she left. The sooner they could clean this up, the sooner she and TJ could figure out what was going on with them.

TJ frowned when his call to Remington went straight to voicemail. It was odd that he couldn't get hold of him. One thing about his former boss, and one thing that probably helped his marriage end, was that Remington always had his phone.

Something must have happened. Something they didn't know about, or it hadn't made it out to the news outlets yet. Remington had heart problems, thanks to the stress of the job and his drinking. And his smoking. Hell, the man was a walking time bomb. If he'd been rushed to the hospital, it wouldn't have made the news. He just wasn't on their radar. But the fact that he had called TJ earlier, but was now not answering, left TJ slightly queasy.

"Hey," he called out as Santos walked by the door. "Have you seen Tsu?"

He shook his head. "He had lunch out. Should be back by now, so I am avoiding him. I want to get out of here on time."

He nodded as is phone rang. Charity. He clicked it on.

"Hey. What's up?"

"I've been trying to get hold of you for awhile now."

"And I've been trying to get hold of Remington. I can't."

"That's odd. The email is even odder. Just says people are onto us. Tells me to flee."

He rolled his shoulders as he stood up so he could pace. "What the hell?"

"Exactly. All a set up. I'm trying to list everything that has happened between the time they say I broke in to steal operative's names, and now. Emma suggested it before she went to the hospital."

"Anything wrong?"

"No. Just baby time."

"Oh." He didn't know what to say to that.

"I was going to wait until you were done with work, if it is going to be soon."

"I need to check in with my boss, then I'll swing by to get you."

"Sounds great."

"Charity."

"Yes."

It had been an easy conversation, and there was no reason to say anything else, but something stuck in the back of his throat. Something he knew he needed to tell her, but wasn't sure how to go about it. Not over the phone.

"We really need to have a talk about us."

There was a long pause—long enough to make the bottom fall out of his stomach.

"I agree, but I think we need to wait until we get through this. Then, I promise, a long chat."

He closed his eyes and ordered his heart to calm down. "Good."

"Just give me a ring when you're at the front door. Everyone else is gone I think. So I am locked up tight in here."

"Will do."

"Bye, TJ."

"Bye, Charity."

Once they were off the phone, he decided to try Remington again, and after no luck, he went in search of his supervisor. It took TJ fifteen minutes before he located Tsu in the break room.

"Hey, Callahan. What's up?"

"I was wondering if you've talked to Remington? I wanted to go over the case since the news this morning."

Tsu frowned. "Didn't he talk to you?"

"What do you mean? He left me a message, but I have not been able to talk to him."

"I thought you two would have lunch or something."

"You're not making any sense."

Tsu blinked. "He's here in Hawaii."

TJ stopped moving, as an icy finger slipped down his spine. "What?"

"Got here last night. Talked to him this morning."

Fear spiked. "What's he doing here?"

"Said something about wanting to talk to that Edwards woman in person."

"I didn't know he was here."

"It's not his first time."

"Wait, what?"

"He was here a couple months ago. I thought he said you two got together."

Something was definitely off. He wasn't afraid right now. He was pissed. All the blocks were starting to fall into place, and he didn't like where they fit.

"Wait, he actually said we got together?"

"Yeah."

"I don't even remember a memo saying he was coming by."

"He didn't come officially." Tsu sighed, and rose from the chair to get more coffee. "He came here because he'd just been served with divorce papers. Or, that is my assumption—I can't really remember. I know he tried to cover up the problems in his marriage for awhile before his wife pushed for divorce. I swear he said he saw you."

"When was it?"

Tsu shrugged. "Couple of months."

He grabbed his supervisor. "When?"

When TJ heard the dates, his heart almost stopped.

"Fuck."

He didn't know what it all meant, but the fact that his mentor had not contacted him was beyond troubling. He started back to his office and pulled out his cell to call Charity, but it went straight to voicemail. He frowned and tried again.

Nothing. That was odd, but he knew there were dead zones at TFH, especially in her lab. Still, something churned in his gut. Something was really off, something bad.

He grabbed his keys and was out the door. He didn't know what the fuck it all meant, but he knew it wasn't good. He just hoped it had nothing to do with Charity.

Charity looked back over her list of occurrences for the last month and sighed. There wasn't much to it, but it all centered around her and TJ. She knew that she didn't do anything to get on the radar of anyone at the FBI. Nothing. The one ripple in the calm waters of TFH was TJ. It all seemed to have something to do with him.

She knew he had nothing to do with setting her up, but was someone setting her up to set him up?

With a groan, she closed her eyes.

"Now you are making no sense, Edwards," she murmured.

Opening her eyes, she sighed. It was best to just close everything down and go to the hospital. She'd been getting texts from the hospital from everyone on the team. The latest was from Graeme, who said Del had passed out at one point and bashed his head. She smiled. She loved when a big old Alpha man fell hard for a woman.

After her computer shut down, she stood, grabbing her pillbox purse. She couldn't wait for the baby. She wasn't one for babies and such, but Emma wasn't the only person who thought of TFH as a family. Emma was like a sister to her, and so she looked at the new baby as her nephew or niece.

There was a footstep in the hallway and her heart jumped. It pounded in her neck. She knew it wasn't anyone from TFH because they were all at the hospital; more than likely causing a ruckus and driving the staff crazy. As a group, they were pretty annoying, she thought with a smile. Couldn't be the cleaning crew. They didn't come in until eight at night.

"Hello? TJ?"

As the silence continued, her nerves stretched tighter.

"TJ?"

Nothing. No word. She tried to call TJ, but her phone was dead. Then, a large man appeared; older, with a bit of gray in his hair, and an unsmiling face. He was wearing a pair of khakis, and the ugliest Hawaiian shirt she had ever seen—and that was saying a lot.

"Sorry, no. Callahan should be here soon, though, but maybe I should introduce myself. Stan Remington."

"TJ's old boss."

He smiled, but there was no humor in it. In fact, there was an gleam to his eyes that could only be described as evil. "Yes, that's right Ms. Edwards." He moved his hand, and it was then she noticed the gun. "But you know me better as Edward Foley."

Chapter Eighteen

Anger and fear rode shotgun on the drive from FBI headquarters to TFH. By the time TJ turned onto Ward Avenue, he was about out of his damned mind. He'd paid no attention to traffic rules and regs. The only thing he cared about was getting to Charity before Remington could hurt her.

His phone buzzed. It had done that several times since he'd started on his way over. He knew it wasn't Charity. Every time, it was Tsu looking for him. The buzzing stopped after a moment.

TJ pulled into the visitor parking behind the building. When he grabbed the phone, he almost growled when he saw it was Tsu, again. He didn't need interference from another FBI supervisor.

He wanted to avoid him, but TJ knew better. His supervisor wasn't going to let it go.

"What?" he snarled.

"Where the fuck are you, Callahan?"

"At TFH. I can't get hold of Charity, and Remington is off the grid."

"Way off the grid. He disappeared from DC yesterday. He just left, no leave. On top of that, there is no record of him coming here."

"Which means he's not here to play nice with anyone."

"And now, he's not answering anything. His phone or email."

"Great."

"I'm calling in HPD, and I'm on my way over there now."

"Gotcha. Treat it as a hostile situation."

"I would rather you wait for us," Tsu said.

"I'd rather you not make me disobey an order."

There was a long beat of silence. "Okay. No orders. We'll be there as fast as we can, and the HPD should get there before us."

TJ clicked off his phone and slipped it into his pocket. After stepping out of his jeep, he grabbed his bulletproof vest. He knew that Tsu had people coming, and the HPD might have been alerted, but for now, he was in charge. He wasn't going to wait.

He approached TFH headquarters with an eye out for anything suspicious. Everything looked normal, eerily so. He knew the team was gone, attending Emma at her delivery, but this felt as if it was too serene. He tried the front door and found it unlocked. He frowned, knowing that Charity had said she was in lockdown. He pulled his gun out of the holster and opened the door. As he walked down the hallway, his phone vibrated. It was Charity.

He turned it on, his heart finally beating normally again.

"Hey, there."

"So nice to hear your voice, Callahan."

Icicles formed in his blood when he heard Remington's voice.

"Remington."

"One of my brightest protégés. You were always quick. It's one of the reasons I liked you, but never trusted you. And you always had wonderful taste in women.

He spoke in a normal voice, as if they were discussing the weather. It was cold-blooded, and that bothered TJ more. That meant Remington thought he was in charge of the situation and, at the moment, TJ was worried that he was.

"Where are you?"

"We are down in Ms. Edward's lab."

Then the line went dead. TJ heard the sirens outside, but ignored them. With dread hanging over him, TJ made his way to the stairwell. Keeping his back to the wall, he walked down the stairs, and made it to Charity's hallway pretty fast. He heard voices, but couldn't make out what they were saying.

Charity almost felt numb. It was like she was in the middle of some horrible movie of the week on Lifetime where her stalker was now going to kill her. She felt as if she were watching it from a distance while she was in the middle of it. And that told her how freaked out she was if she wasn't making sense in her own head.

Her captor hadn't said much. He'd muttered plenty, but very little of it seemed to make sense. He'd used the gun to force her to sit down while he used plastic cuffs to restrain her. She knew from her training, the best thing to do was to engage him. If she could get him talking, he would be distracted, and that would help TJ.

She closed her eyes as terror screamed through her system. Just thinking his name had her losing her sanity. She couldn't think of him. Not now. She knew he was on his way down, but she had to put him out of her head. If she didn't, she would surely panic.

"Have you even thought this through?" Charity asked.

He snorted. "Yes. You have no idea how long I have been planning this."

She didn't really want to know. The thought that a man TJ looked up to, thought of as a mentor, was capable of doing this just made her sick. She could only imagine what this was going to do to him. At the moment, he would be ready to kill Remington for threatening her. Knowing that Remington had used that trust to commit crimes was going to tear TJ's heart out.

"Tell us, how long have you been planning it?"

TJ was standing there in the doorway, as big as day. Relief came first, leaving her almost dizzy, but then, she realized he was a target. Anger and fear came rushing back. What the hell, was he standing there waiting to get shot? He had a bulletproof vest on, but that didn't protect his head. The idiot was going to get himself killed.

"First, let's drop the weapon there. On the ground."

He didn't pay any attention to Remington. His gaze moved to her. "How are you doing, Charity? Did he hurt you?"

"No."

Something must have eased his worry because his expression lightened. She watched as TJ dropped his gun on the floor.

"Kick it over here."

TJ did as Remington ordered, but the slight tightening around his mouth told her that he wasn't happy with having to do it. Of course, he wasn't. He was virtually unarmed now. TJ didn't carry a lot of weapons on him, and that was probably the only one he kept with him throughout the work day. Why did he need weapons? He was a cyber geek.

"That's a good little FBI agent." The gleeful tone to Remington's voice made Charity's stomach turn over. "And, to answer your question: Years. Of course, this little bit was last minute, or I should say, the last six months."

"Why?"

"Why would anyone do something like this? Money." Then Remington snorted. "Of course, *Captain America* wouldn't understand that. Too much pride for that, right, Callahan?"

"No. It's the fact that my parents raised me right."

Another snort, but she felt the barrel of the gun ease back from her temple.

"Sure, sure, the sainted Callahans." Sarcasm replaced the glee and Charity welcomed it. She could handle that over someone being happy about deceiving and planning to kill TJ. "Well, after twenty years, I was ready for a new start, for something all mine."

"You killed people. Ruined lives."

She didn't dare look at Remington, but she felt his shrug. "They were stupid, and many of them had already been committing crimes on their own. I just helped the FBI take them down for something else."

Charity watched TJ's jaw flex, telling her he was grinding his teeth. Remington probably knew his comments would get to TJ and was using it to hurt him. That made her want to hurt the bastard even more.

"So, what is going to happen here?"

"Ah, yes, the plan. You were always one with a plan, weren't you, Callahan? Hell, you have lists and lists of shit to do in your head, don't you?"

"At one time, you thought that made me a good FBI agent."

Another snort. "It made you easy to control. You wanted so badly to be accepted on merit that you would do anything to get it."

"Being prepared and being good at my job have nothing to do with that."

"Sure, Callahan. I'm sure you have no daddy issues, right? That your need to succeed at the FBI wasn't to prove to everyone you were better than your father."

"No. No daddy issues, other than the fact I was raised to do the right thing. Apparently, you weren't."

Remington grunted, but didn't say anything else.

"Your plan now?"

"Well, my plan is to kill Ms. Edwards."

Her stomach churned, and she had to swallow bile that had risen into her throat. She knew that had been his objective, or at least some facsimile of it. But hearing it expressed out loud left her physically ill.

TJ, once again, remained cool under pressure. "What is that going to get you?"

"You'll take the fall. I've done enough to plant the information. Dangled her out in front of you like a prime piece of meat. She is definitely your type."

The anger and fear that had been dominating her feelings now had a healthy dose of irritation. She might be forced to take some maniac with a gun, but she would not be put into a category.

"What do you mean by that? I am not a *type*. I am an individual."

Remington pressed the barrel harder against her temple.

"Charity," TJ said, exasperation filling his tone.

Remington went on. "You are *definitely* his type. Smart, pretty, a little on the curvy side. He likes a woman with a little spirit in her. You were perfect, and you were easy to set up. So easy. Now, it will look like you were working for him, and he was the one who was calling the shots."

TJ shook his head and stepped a little closer. It was then that she realized he had been inching forward for the last couple of minutes.

"You can't get away with it. Cops are on their way."

"You think I don't know how to stage a scene? After all this time, are you really still that naïve?"

TJ said nothing. He kept staring at Remington, and she could see his mind working. TJ never sat back and let things happen. He would plan, and then he would execute the plan. Right now, he was figuring something out in his head.

"Nothing? You have nothing to say?" Remington's voice had raised to a shout.

TJ shrugged, pretending indifference. At least, she was hoping he was pretending indifference. If he wasn't, she might just kill him if they got out of this.

Then, without looking at her, TJ said, "Don't move, Charity."

Before she could blink, TJ rushed Remington. Remington turned, swung the gun in TJ's direction, but there wasn't time for him to shoot. TJ tackled him, and they went falling to the floor. She jumped out of the chair and searched for something, anything to hit Remington with. They rolled around, punches being thrown, and TJ got in a few before she heard the gun go off.

Fury and terror exploded within her. With a scream, she grabbed an award she had won when she worked for the CIA. It was metal, and she knew it would hurt. Remington turned toward her, and she whacked him across the face with the figurine. He fell back, his hand hitting the credenza, causing him to lose the gun. Charity paid no attention to where it went. Remington was trying to regain his balance, so she concentrated on him instead. Without full use of her hands, since they were still restrained, she used what she knew from defensive training, and what her mother had taught her. She lifted her knee and hit him in the face. The sound of crushing bone left a sick pit in her stomach, but she ignored it. She had to make sure he stayed down.

"Bastard. You do not hurt *my* man, and I am *definitely* not a type."

She was still kicking him when she felt hands on her arms. She spun around, ready to attack, but found it was TJ.

"Hey, babe, calm down. He's unconscious, I think."

"If not, I'll make him wish he was," she said, biting out every word as she turned to kick him again.

"It's okay. We're safe."

His steady voice calmed her nerves. He grabbed a pair of

scissors from her desk and cut her restraints. The normalcy of his actions calmed her down, until she looked at him. He sported a split lip, and blood stained his white shirt on one shoulder.

"You're hurt."

He shook his head, then winced. "Damn, that..."

His words trailed off, and his face lost a lot of color. He closed his eyes and swallowed. Charity knew that he was probably trying his best not to throw up. Before she could say anything else, police and FBI were pouring into her office. With them, she saw Adam and Marcus.

"You really know how to throw a party, Charity," Marcus said with a smile. "Whoa, Callahan, you don't look so good."

"I'm jusss fine."

She shook her head, feeling slightly off center herself. She knew the adrenaline was starting to dissipate. "You are not fine. The bastard shot you."

"Tis nothing but a flesh wound."

"Sit down." She helped him into the chair in which she had been held hostage. "Where are the medics? Did someone call?"

Before anyone could answer her, EMTs came rushing into the office. There were two, a large Hawaiian man she'd seen before, but didn't really know. The woman of the pair was someone Charity had talked to before; although, she couldn't remember the woman's name. She was a head shorter than the man, but definitely in charge.

"You need to get out of the way," the female EMT said.

Charity hesitated, then after one more squeeze to TJ's hand, she stepped back.

As the EMT's started to work on TJ, she turned and saw

an FBI agent cuffing Remington. He didn't look so threatening now. They gave him a tissue to hold against his bleeding nose—which she was sure she had broken—and he definitely was going to have some massive bruising on his face.

Then, in one split second, he raised his gaze to hers. He snarled his lip, and then lunged in her direction as he screeched. Her heart jumped into her throat, but she fisted her hand just in case he got close enough for her to punch him. He didn't get far. FBI Agents grabbed him and held him back. But, before she knew what he was doing, TJ was standing in front of her as if to protect her again. He swayed a little bit, but he stood there waiting until they pulled him back. It was then she realized there was blood on the back of his head.

"You stay the fuck away from her, Remington. If you ever get close or even think of hurting her again, I will tear you into so many pieces, they will not be able to identify your body."

The agents tugged on Remington hard, and then gave up and dragged him out of the office.

"His head is bleeding," she told the EMTs, who were tugging him back into the chair.

"I see that," the female EMT said. She inspected it, then pulled out a light. "Look at me, Agent Callahan."

He did as ordered.

"It doesn't look like you have a concussion, but I think we need to make sure."

"Is he going to be okay?"

"Yes, but we need to get him to the hospital. Better safe than sorry."

"It's a flesh wound," TJ repeated again.

"Which hospital?"

"They said to transport him to Queen's. Get the stretcher," she said, ordering the other EMT to get it.

"Well, that works out," Adam said. "That's where the Boss and Emma are."

She had completely forgotten that the first TFH baby was on the way. "Did she have it yet?"

Marcus shook his head. "Not yet, and Del is a mess. He came out and gave us a few updates. White as a sheet. He apparently passed out once in the delivery room."

For the first time in what felt like a lifetime, she smiled. "Oh, my God."

Marcus laughed and nodded. "Elle had to replace him for a while. When we got the call, he was holding steady from all reports."

The gurney arrived, and they worked to get TJ loaded onto it. All the while, he complained that he could walk, but his words didn't always make sense.

"I'm riding along with him."

Both of the EMTs turned to look at her, and the male opened his mouth, apparently to tell her no. The female stopped him.

"Okay, but don't get in the way."

Within fifteen minutes, they were on their way to the hospital. They had administered an IV, and TJ had his eyes closed.

"Hey, Charity."

His voice didn't really sound like him. His words were a little slurred, as if he had been drinking. She looked at the EMT, who smiled. "We gave him a little something for the pain. So right now, he might be a little goofy. With no sign of concussion, I wanted to ease the headache that is probably about to hit him."

Charity nodded.

"Charrrrrity."

She laughed, and he opened his eyes. Her chest loosened, as the rest of the fear dissolved. She had been in a panic from the moment Remington had appeared, but now she knew they were both safe and that the nightmare was over.

"What?" she asked.

He crooked his finger to urge her closer. She complied, thinking he would whisper. He didn't. He shouted in her ear.

"Don't tell anyone my name is Thor."

The EMT looked at her with her eyebrows up and mouthed *Thor*. Charity nodded.

He frowned and somehow made himself more attractive. "Promise."

"I promise," she said, kissing his forehead.

His expression brightened. "That's what I love about you. You're pretty and smart. And pretty."

"Thank you."

He had one eye closed, and he watched her with the other one. It was as if he was trying to figure out if she were real.

"Woman."

"What?"

"You know I love you, right?"

Before she could answer him, he passed out. She stared at him for a long moment. "TJ?"

He didn't answer.

"He's probably out."

Constant Craving

Charity looked at the EMT. "Is he okay?"

The EMT moved closer and pulled up one of TJ's eyelids to check his response to light. "Yes. The drugs probably helped him along, because he only lost a little blood. He was right. It was a flesh wound, but we need to clean it up, and he might need a stitch or two, also, we need to double check that head. The most pain he will probably have is from the headache, like I said."

She sighed in relief. "Thank you."

"His name is really Thor?"

Charity nodded. "His parents are Marvel freaks."

And he loved her.

That was enough for now.

Chapter Nineteen

Charity was relieved when it didn't take long to get TJ fixed up. As the EMT had said, it was a flesh wound and required just a few stitches. They had rushed to get a cat scan, which had come back negative. His clothes had to go into evidence, so the hospital had given him a set of scrubs. He'd had no trouble with the pants, but after watching him for several moments struggle with the top, she stepped forward and helped him. The moment she was within grabbing distance he became amazingly agile with his hands.

She laughed as he made a grab for her rear end. "Stop that."

When she finally got the top on him, she moved back. He opened his mouth just as his phone buzzed. He grabbed it and tried to punch in his code.

"My fingers are broken. Or my phone is."

She took it from him. "How much more of those drugs did they give you?"

When she looked down at the screen, she found a picture

of Black Widow with the name Mom on the ID. Damn, it was his mother.

"Hey." He said, frowning at her. Then, he smiled. "Have I told you that you're pretty?"

"Only about twenty times. Give me your code."

He rattled off the code, and she answered his phone. "Hello."

There was a long silence. "I was trying to get hold of TJ Callahan."

"This is his phone. My name is—"

"Charity," she said, and she could hear the smile in his mother's voice. "My other boys have told me about you."

"Other boys?"

"TJ's brothers. And, I did hear about the first date. My name is Jen Callahan. Is TJ around?"

"He is, but you might not want to talk to him. He had a little mishap, and they had to give him some drugs."

"Oh, God."

The horror in his mother's voice made Charity regret her blunt comment. She rushed to reassure Jen. "Nothing bad. They don't even want to keep him overnight."

"No, I was talking about the drugs. TJ can be brutally honest on painkillers. It can be funny—but it can also be painful."

"Who is on my phone?" TJ asked, trying to grab it from her.

"Your mother."

"Did you tell her that I think you're pretty? Because I do."

"We haven't gotten to that part yet."

Constant Craving

His mother was laughing when she spoke next. "Let me talk to my boy."

Charity handed the phone to him. "Hey, Mama."

He was quiet for a little bit. "Just a flesh wound. Have I told you that she is pretty?"

Another long silence. "Yes. She is nice. I haven't said anything mean. I told her she was pretty."

He smiled at her, then winked, as his mother continued to chatter in his ear.

"Okay. I'll call tomorrow."

Then he clicked the phone off. "That was my Mama. She said you sounded nice, and she would box my ears if I said mean things."

"And how will she know?"

TJ frowned. "Not sure, but she always seems to know. She's got superpowers."

She laughed that was close to a pout. "I think all mothers have that superpower."

"I'm all ready to go, right?"

She nodded. "If you are up to it, I need to go upstairs. Everyone is up there."

"I can handle anything. I'm in the FBI. But why is everyone there?"

"Emma's having her baby. Remember?"

"Oh. Babies. Don't know much about them. Do you?"

She shook her head.

"I think you should have my babies."

It was the third time he had told her that, so she just nodded. She knew there was a ninety-nine percent chance he would not remember any of this in the morning.

269

Just then, his supervisor Tsu came through the door. "Hey, there. They tell me you are all good."

"I'm the best."

Tsu looked at her. She shrugged. "Painkillers."

"Ah. Okay. I take it you can get him home?"

She nodded.

"Tell him that he can take the next week off, but he might be called in for his report. Hell, make it two weeks."

"I'm right here."

"Yes, you are, but I have a feeling you aren't going to remember any of this," Tsu said. "Call if you need anything, Ms. Edwards."

"I will. Thank you."

"No, I think you deserve the thanks. This is one big mess, and the FBI is definitely going to get some flak for it in the press—not to mention DC. The fact that you and Callahan worked together on it, and he figured it out...we are in your debt. I understand you broke Remington's nose?"

She nodded.

"Good. That man was always kind of a self-righteous bastard. I respected his work, but he always acted like he was better than the rest of us. Those types are usually the ones who commit the worst crimes." He sighed. "Again, please let us know if there is anything you need."

As Tsu left, an orderly came in with a wheelchair. Charity had asked for one earlier, so it would be easier to get him upstairs for a short check-in with Emma.

The orderly helped her get TJ into the chair, then she wheeled him out to the elevator. Maternity was on the tenth floor. As soon as the elevator doors opened, she saw the team. They were all sitting there waiting.

"Hey, it's the team," TJ yelled. They all turned to look at them.

"This is going to be interesting," she murmured, as she wheeled him down the hall to the team.

"How are you doing, Callahan?" Adam asked.

"Fine and dandy. Fine and dandy. Who's having a baby?"

"Emma," she said. "He's a little out of it thanks to the painkillers."

Adam chuckled. "It's good to know you're doing okay. No concussion?"

She shook her head. "And thanks to your cousin, they rushed him through so I could get him home. Any word?"

"I was just in there a little while ago," Elle said. "She was about there, so hopefully, any time now."

As if on cue, the doors opened and Del came striding out. She leaned closer to Adam. "Did he really pass out?"

"Yeah, and we have it on video."

Del smiled when he spotted them and rushed over. "It's a girl."

As everyone congratulated him, his gaze zeroed in on TJ. "Hey, I heard something went down."

TJ said nothing for once. She looked down and found him sleeping. "He had some meds."

He nodded. She gave Del a hug and kissed him on the cheek. "Congrats, Daddy."

He pulled back and looked down at her. "Thanks. You better get him home. Adam might need to help you."

She nodded. "What are you naming her?"

"Evangeline Michelle."

"Oh," she said, as her eyes started to burn. "That's so pretty."

He gave her a kiss on the cheek. "I guess I should get back in there. They said we can have visitors pretty soon."

Adam stepped up next to her as Del walked away. "Ready?"

She nodded. "I would love to stay and see that baby, but I need to get him into bed so he can rest. Let's go."

It took them a few minutes to get TJ into the TFH SUV. By the time they got to her apartment, TJ was sort of awake and could walk. Still, Adam stayed and helped get him up to her apartment and into bed.

"He's going to hurt tomorrow."

"Yes, but I'm pretty sure he'll not admit it, and refuse the prescription the doc gave him."

Adam slanted her a look. "How do you know that?"

"He's a stupid boy. You are all the same. Stoically refuse to admit you are in pain." She kissed Adam's cheek. "Thanks for the help now and earlier."

"Callahan apparently had it under control."

She smiled. "You are a good man, Adam Lee."

His humor faded and she hated that. "Yeah, well, not so sure about that."

"I forgot to ask what happened with Jin."

He rubbed his hand over his bald head. "I told her if she didn't go to rehab, I would stop checking on her."

"And?"

"She went in today. Good place. They specialize in abuse survivors."

"That's good. Right?"

He nodded, but he didn't look any happier. "I feel like I betrayed her."

"Oh, Adam, you didn't. You were the one friend who stood by her. She needs this, and one day she'll see that."

He stared unseeing down the hall, then he turned back to her. He really was a sweet man.

"I hope so."

She rose to her tiptoes and gave him another kiss on the cheek. "As I said before, you are a good man. Call me if you need someone to talk to."

He finally gave her a small smile. "Callahan is pretty damned lucky."

"I know, right? Night, Adam."

"Night."

She sighed as she locked her door, and then made her way back to the bedroom. He was laying there, still wearing the scrubs the ER had given him. She decided to get ready for bed. Stripping out of her clothes, she pulled on her favorite PJ shorts and top. She stepped back into her room and stared. He was okay. Everything was all over and neither of them had any major injuries. Then, as if she realized that it was okay to break, she did. Tears welled up in her eyes and, before she knew what was happening, a sob escaped from her mouth. She covered it with her hand, but it was too late. TJ woke up.

"Charity?"

"Sorry. I didn't mean to wake you."

"Come here."

She hesitated, then did as he asked. After curling up next to him, she continued to cry. He said nothing, just wrapped his arm around her. By the time the crying jag was over, she was exhausted.

"You'll be here in the morning?" he asked.

She frowned at the stupid question, but she realized he might just be out of it still. "Yeah, I'll be here."

"Good."

His breathing evened out, and she could tell he was sleeping again. Drained by the day's events and the crying jag, she drifted off with the warmth of TJ's body warming her and the beat of his heart lulling her into slumber.

Sun slanting through the blinds woke TJ the next morning. He tried to ignore it, to go back to sleep. He tried to roll over, then cussed as searing pain shot from his shoulder. He rubbed his hand over his eyes and looked around. He was in Charity's room, but she was not there.

With care, he rose from bed. The room seemed to revolve around him suddenly. His head pounded and almost had him throwing up. He closed his eyes and steadied himself.

"Hey, you should have called me," Charity said.

He opened his eyes, as she rushed over to slip one of his arms over her shoulders.

"I had control of the situation." He bit out every word.

Charity didn't say anything. Instead, she just helped him to the bathroom. When she made a move to follow him in, he shook his head and immediately regretted it. Fuck. Who put rocks in his head?

"I can handle this on my own."

She didn't look like she believed him, but she let him go.

Constant Craving

"Call if you need me," she said before she closed the bathroom door behind her.

He relieved himself, then washed up. When he looked at himself in the mirror, he cringed. His face was pale, and there were dark circles under his eyes. It hadn't been that bad of an injury, but apparently his thirty-five-year old body wasn't able to bounce back that easily.

He pulled off the blue scrubs shirt and looked at the bandage. It looked good, no blood showed. While it hurt, it was from movement, not from the wound itself. He hoped there was no infection.

Drawing in a deep breath, he prepared himself to go back out into the bedroom. He hated that she was seeing him like this, weak, as if he couldn't take care of himself.

He opened the door and found her sitting on the bed. "Ready for some coffee and time on the lanai?"

He nodded, but then shook his head when she acted as if she was going to help him out into the living room. "I can handle it."

She frowned, but she allowed him his space. She followed him out, then grabbed two cups and the thermal coffee pot. He sat down, and she set the cups on the table and poured the coffee.

"How are you feeling?"

"Like crap."

She smiled and sat down. "I have your meds."

"How did you get those?"

"It helps that Adam is related to so many people at the hospital. His cousin set you up with the antibiotics, and there are a few painkillers too."

"Everything is kind of fuzzy."

"Yeah, well, you apparently don't handle painkillers well," she said, looking out at the traffic below them. She was avoiding making eye contact.

Damn, he had a really bad habit of being brutally honest with people when he was high on painkillers.

"Charity?"

"Hmm?"

"Did I say anything horrible?"

She shook her head.

"Then why won't you look at me?"

She glanced at him, then away. "You were sweet, and you told me I was pretty. A lot. Tsu stopped by and told you to take the next week off. They'll call you and keep you updated."

"Remington?"

"Arrested, but more than likely working out some kind of deal. You know how that goes."

He grunted.

"You also talked to your mother."

"Shit."

"It was all okay. I reassured her that you were fine, that it was nothing to worry about."

"Thanks. I guess I'll have to call her today."

"You do need to because you said you would. I already talked to my folks about what happened. I was afraid it would make the news."

He nodded, but there was something still there, something she wasn't tell him.

"Charity. There's something else."

She shook her head and smiled at him. "No."

Then, bits and pieces of the night before came back to

him. Charity beating the crap out of Remington, the ride in the ambulance...

"Charity? Did I say something on the way to the hospital?"

"You told me I was pretty."

He narrowed his eyes as he studied her. She was trying not to laugh.

"Tell me the truth."

Her eyes widened. "I *am* telling you the truth. Unless you think it isn't true that I'm pretty."

He opened his mouth to refute that, but he caught the gleam in her eyes. "Do not try that crap on me. I said something else in the ambulance."

"Okay, okay. You told me you loved me."

Well, shit. He hadn't meant to tell her. Not right now. It was too early, and they had been wrapped up in the investigation.

"Oh."

She cleared her throat, and he waited for it. The brushoff. He knew her history with men, and he had really made a fucking muck of things. He'd rushed it, and while women like the "l" word, it was too fast. He probably came off as a creep.

"I was on drugs, so it doesn't count."

"Really? Because your mother told me you are usually brutally honest when you are drugged up."

He was going to kill his mother. No, he wasn't. But he might talk to her sternly. Scratch that. His mother was kind of scary when she was pissed at them, so he would just tell her not to tell people that anymore. Maybe.

"She's got a drinking problem."

Charity gave him a look of disgust. "Thor Jackson Callahan. Do you want me to call your mother and tell her about what you said?"

"Shit. No."

Charity's expression softened. "My mama always said to trust a man who has a healthy fear of his own mother."

He shook his head. "I didn't mean to tell you."

Her eyes widened. "You weren't going to tell me you loved me? Ever?"

"No." She frowned. "I mean, I was going to tell you. I was going to ease you into it."

"Ease me into it."

"Yeah. Get you used to the idea that I was in love with you. I know everything is moving fast, and we had the investigation."

"Yeah, there was that."

"So, I didn't want to scare you off with professions of love."

"Makes sense. But, you told me in front of the EMT. Oh, and you also told me not to tell anyone your name is Thor."

"In front of the EMT?"

She nodded as her mouth curved. "She was impressed, but I think your days of keeping that little secret hidden are over."

"I think I really will kill my mother for giving me that name."

There was a long silence, and Charity cleared her throat.

"Are you freaking out?" he asked.

She shrugged. "So, you love me?"

He nodded, waiting. Sure, she wouldn't kick him out today. He'd gotten wounded helping her. But, as Del had said, Charity wasn't one for long term. She would nurse him back to health, then the freak out would take over, and she would slowly put distance between them. Well, he wasn't having it. He loved her, and she was stuck with him.

"Just so you know, I'm not budging. I love you, and I am not going anywhere."

"Well, that's good," she said as she took his hand. "Because I love you."

For a moment, he didn't think he heard her correctly. Then her words set in. His heart lightened as he felt his lips start to curve.

"Yeah?"

She nodded. He tugged on her hand and pulled her out of her chair, and then onto his lap.

"TJ, be careful of your arm."

"It's fine."

She cupped his face, as the laughter faded from her golden brown eyes. "I was so worried when you got shot. I thought I was going to lose you."

"Did you beat Remington over the head with one of your awards?"

She laughed. "Yeah, I did. Then I broke his nose."

"That's my woman."

"I do love you, Thor Jackson Callahan."

"And I love you, Charity Frederica Edwards."

"Frederica is not my middle name."

"At the moment, Howard could be your middle name and I wouldn't care."

She kissed him. In that one kiss, he could feel her emotions roll over him. The fear of the day before, the love she felt for him. It spread through him, warmed his heart, and soothed his soul. He returned the kiss with enthusiasm. When he pulled back, she had tears in her eyes.

"Don't cry," he said, brushing away one tear that escaped.

"I'm sorry. It has been a rollercoaster lately. It still gets to me."

He gave her one long kiss again, then eased her off his lap and stood. He took her hand and tugged her off the lanai and toward the bedroom.

"How about we spend the day in bed?"

She shook her head, but she came along easily. "You are supposed to get some rest."

"That wasn't exactly what I had in mind." He wiggled his eyebrows, and pulled her into his arms at the foot of the bed. He nuzzled her neck and drew in her scent. This was it. This was home.

She shook her head. "You need your rest."

He pulled back and looked at her. "We'll get rest. Later."

She was laughing when they fell onto the bed together.

Mahalo for reading CONSTANT CRAVING. If you enjoyed Charity and TJ's story, please consider leaving a review at your favorite retailer or review site.

Next up is Cat and Drew in TANGLED PASSIONS.

Facing an obsessive killer proves to be easier than falling in love.

You can never go wrong with the Task Force Hawaii Team!

1-click—>TANGLED PASSIONS!

Acknowledgments

I always say that no book is ever written by one person alone. Without the support I have in my personal and professional life, I would never finish a book.

Thanks to Noelle Varner for her hard work on the edits as always and a big thanks to Brandy Walker for stepping up and creating such a beautiful cover. Thanks to the Addicts for being around for years and always supporting my publishing efforts.

And last but not least, thanks to my family for always being there.

About the Author

From an early age, USA Today Bestselling author Melissa loved to read. When she discovered the romance genre, she started to listen to the voices in her head. After years of following her AF Major husband around, she is happy to be settled in Northern Virginia surrounded by horses, wineries, and many, many Wegmans.

Keep up with Mel, her releases, and her appearances by subscribing to her NEWSLETTER or join in the fun with her Harmless Addicts!

Check out all her other books, family trees and other info at her website!
If you would want contact Mel, email her at:
melissa@melissaschroeder.net

- instagram.com/melschro
- amazon.com/author/melissa_schroeder
- facebook.com/MelissaSchroederfanpage
- twitter.com/melschroeder
- bookbub.com/authors/melissa-schroeder
- goodreads.com/Melissa_Schroeder

Printed in Great Britain
by Amazon